ASCENDING

THE

BONEYARD

ASCENDING

THE

BONEYARD

C. G. WATSON

SIMON PULSE
New York   London   Toronto   Sydney   New Delhi

SIMON PULSE

An imprint of Simon & Schuster Children's Publishing Division

1230 Avenue of the Americas, New York, New York 10020

First Simon Pulse hardcover edition February 2016

Text copyright © 2016 by C.G. Watson

Jacket photograph copyright © 2016 by Oliver Charles/Arcangel Images

All rights reserved, including the right of reproduction in whole or in part in any form.

SIMON PULSE and colophon are registered trademarks of Simon & Schuster, Inc.

For information about special discounts for bulk purchases, please contact Simon & Schuster Special Sales at 1-866-506-1949 or business@simonandschuster.com.

The Simon & Schuster Speakers Bureau can bring authors to your live event.

For more information or to book an event contact the Simon & Schuster Speakers Bureau at 1-866-248-3049 or visit our website at www.simonspeakers.com.

Jacket designed by Regina Flath

Interior designed by Tom Daly

The text of this book was set in Weiss Std.

Manufactured in the United States of America

2 4 6 8 10 9 7 5 3 1

Library of Congress Cataloging-in-Publication Data

Watson, C. G.

Ascending the boneyard / by C. G. Watson. — First Simon Pulse hardcover edition.

p. cm.

Summary: Overwhelmed by a series of losses, including an accident that left his brother in a wheelchair, his father's abuse, and his mother's departure, sixteen-year-old Tosh escapes into a video game, but soon the game becomes much more real than his life.

[1. Virtual reality—Fiction. 2. Video games—Fiction. 3. Family problems—Fiction. 4. Loss (Psychology)—Fiction. 5. Brothers—Fiction. 6. People with disabilities—Fiction.] I. Title.

PZ7.1.W415Asc 2016

[Fic]—dc23

2014049485

ISBN 978-1-4814-3184-2 (hc)

ISBN 978-1-4814-3186-6 (eBook)

For Argo . . .

who heard

who saw

who knew

ASCENDING THE BONEYARD

- .5 -

Everything's a battle.

The way my brother Devin and I always fought for space and attention, from the second he was born up until the accident.

The constant slaughter and resurrection of cockroaches in every rotting corner of our trailer.

The old man at max volume, having it out with my mom for the 1,586th day in a row. Ever since the accident. Every single day.

Scratching day-old mac-n-cheese and dried beer foam out of his stubble as he rants. Such an ass, I can't even think of him as my dad anymore.

Haze was there. He knows what it's like to have to live with that kind of memory. Thinks I'm stuck on that one day at the go-karts, that it's still breaking me down after four years. Thinks I'm gonna get lost in the game.

"You need to get off the computer," he says, as if that'll fix everything.

He doesn't play, so he doesn't get it.

Doesn't get that I actually feel like I can do something meaningful in the Boneyard. Y'know?

Free the hostages.

Kill the roaches.

Become Worthy.

Ascend.

– 1 –

Saturday afternoon, Cam Tyler bursts into my room like it's a matter of national security.

"You gotta try these, man. They're off the hook!"

I'm barely awake, but I slip the specs from his hand. By all appearances, they're ordinary goggles with a yellow tint to the lens. I cut him one of those sidewinder looks.

"No one says 'off the hook' anymore," I tell him, throwing my legs over the side of the bed, kicking a dirty cup and plate out of the way as I head to the desk.

"My dad does."

"Your dad thinks he's the long-lost drummer for KISS, dude. He's an eighties throwback. Of course he's gonna say 'off the hook.'"

Cam hops around my chair, pushing his long, curly hair out of his freckled face. "Fire up the Boneyard, dude! Try 'em out."

I go to put the glasses on, but he balls his pasty hand into a fist and punches me in the shoulder.

"No, wait! Put 'em on *after* you're in the Boneyard. So you can tell the difference."

That, of course, will mean waiting at least five minutes until the rickety, limping carcass of a Dell PC in my room—the Relic, I call it—coughs itself back to life. I rub my arm in the meantime.

Cam fills the dead space with an endless spew of chatter.

Out front, the old man barks about the mail, like he's incapable of walking twenty-five feet to get it himself.

My eyes blur as I stare at the computer screen, waiting, blocking out the noise from the TV in the front room. I can hear Devin banging through the cardboard-grade wall that separates our rooms, feel the entire trailer rattle as my mom paces the back end of the hallway. The energy outside my room feels like just before an UnderWorld raid—all the crackle and sulfur of unleashed rage and the fear that everything's about to blow wide open.

I have a couple more minutes of wait time till the computer boots up.

"Don't touch anything," I tell Cam. "I'll be right back."

I ease the door open and hook a quick U-turn into Devin's room. He's pounding on the tray of his wheelchair.

"Hey," I say, low and soft so he doesn't spook. "Hey, it's all cool, kid. Your cup's right here."

I'm careful not to cover up the Batman logo on the side of the cup as I hold the sippy part against his lips. He hated Batman before the accident. *Any ten-year-old who likes superheroes is an assnugget,* he'd say.

Now it's the only cup he'll drink from.

Half the water goes into his mouth. The other half slides down his chin. I pat him dry with a soft cloth, pretending it's all water and no drool.

"You probably wanna go watch TV, huh?" I say. He can't nod or anything, but in my mind he does. "Maybe later," I say. "After the old man calms down a little. Okay, kid? Want me to put some music on?"

He'd nod if he could—I know it—so I hit the power button on the radio, tune it back to the emo station he always listened to. The old man changes it to country every freakin' chance he gets. Can't even let Devin have this one little thing.

I smooth my brother's hair down before heading back to my room.

When I get there, Cam holds his hands up like proof he didn't touch anything. Which of course tells me he most likely did.

As soon as I sit back down, the Relic sputters itself into existence and I head straight for the Boneyard. I click the skull-and-crossbones icon, the one with the bullet-riddled military helmet that spins as the game loads agonizingly slow.

Suddenly my character screen blazes into existence, and massive relief washes over me. I pick T-Man, my only level-cap toon, and enter.

More waiting.

Out in the living room, the old man switches channels. Something ridiculous. *Promzillas*, if I had to guess.

On-screen, the load bar crawls past so slowly I want to punch something.

Cam yammers on about how I need a new computer, maybe an Alienware, like I have three large lying around under my mattress.

And then, finally, I'm in.

T-Man drops onto a dark road, and as soon as he's on the move, I put the glasses on.

"Whoa . . ."

"See? Right? See what I mean? It's sick, man, it's totally sick!"

I have to admit, they're pretty cool. Edges are sharper, colors are clearer, and there's almost a 3-D depth to scenery on-screen.

Comments fly by in the chat window, glowing and totally readable, not the blur it usually is. Raids are firing up everywhere. Everybody wants a piece of this battle, especially the special-bonus armor and the max-damage weps that drop if your platoon rocks UpRising.

I keep my eyes plastered to the screen, my hand near but not on the mouse. Close enough to touch if I have to.

Watch the comments fly by.

Psychobatter's on about some dumb bullshit. I wouldn't raid with that guy if I had to. He's an idiot.

Supershooter says he needs a shield tank. Super's in Tenth Warriors—pretty awesome platoon. Maybe I should drop in with them. But no. I promised Haze no raiding. Raiding's where I get a little lost sometimes.

Deathtoaliens claims 10/12 for UpRising.

LAST TUNNEL—need dps.

Last tunnel? Shit on a stick—somebody's that close? Wait a

second. Death? Death's in Doomstalkers—that's *my* brigade.

Since when does Doomstalkers have a group that close to kicking UpRising?

I adjust the goggles, squint closely at the monitor. Seriously though. It's crazy how something so simple brings everything else into such intense focus.

Just when I think it can't get any cooler, I hear the old man squawk, "How many times are they gonna send us the same damn bills?" and suddenly my brigade chat window goes batshit crazy.

Deathtoaliens: T-Man! You in?

Bruisedozer: T-Man, dude, bring the heat.

Sixkindsofwhoopazz: T-Maaaaaaan!

"These are dope," I tell Cam about the goggles, distracting myself so I'm not tempted to get pulled into the action.

My hands are adrenaline-shaking as the raid invites pop up. Eleven people, all begging for me to join. They need me to help break through to that last tunnel, take down the boss. We could do this, no question. It could be *our* screenshot on the forums. With one incomparable grenade launcher, I could kill anything in the game.

"My dad bought two pairs of those goggles," Cam says. I just bet he did. One for Cam and one for himself, no doubt. The guy's a sixteen-year-old trapped in a thirty-five-year-old body.

My finger twitches, and before I know what I'm doing, I click "join." I try not to pay attention to everybody's typing as the lines fly by, players telling me how we're gonna crack this now that I'm back in, names I mostly know and a few I don't. But of course I

7

know Bruisedozer, who's handing off rations, and Six, who's buff-ing everybody like crazy.

The walls shake as my mom paces the narrow hall, and I wish one of those buffs could go to her. She needs something today, I can tell.

"Hold up. I thought this one got paid." Only the way he says it sounds like an accusation.

I hate him for the way he talks to her. Every day. Ever since the accident. Sometimes I wish she'd get angry back. But she knows better, talks to him like she's reading how to reheat soup off the side of a can.

"You're drifting, dude," Cam says.

I turn back to the screen. Behind the raid, a horde of mobs sweeps up and down the street, up and down. Christ, that's a lot of cockroaches. Bruise is going over strategy on voice chat like always—drones on forever before anybody gets to start shooting.

"So what's the point of these, exactly?" I ask, slipping the goggles back off, inspecting them.

"Cuts the glare so you can game longer," Cam says.

I'm totally down for hanging out in the Boneyard all night and helping Doomstalkers take UpRising. Only at that exact second, Haze comes cruising into my room, still sporting the cop shades and painter's mask he wears for work that got him affectionately dubbed the "Napoleon Burger Unabomber." No one twirls a sign like my man Haze.

I try to body block the screen so he can't tell that I'm break-ing a promise to him about getting off the Boneyard. *You're gonna lose yourself in that game one of these days,* he keeps telling me.

My hand goes limp on the mouse.

Haze toggles his mirror-lensed gaze from me to Cam.

"What's going on?" he asks.

Cam and I both answer, only he says "Boneyard" and I say "Nothing," and it's obvious Haze believes Cam and not me.

My hand bumps off the mute by mistake, and now he can hear the raid chat and Bruise yelling that this time they better keep the tank from getting crushed under all those roaches.

"You guys need to get your story straight," Haze mumbles in disgust, aiming those mirrored cop shades straight at me. "I thought you were off that shit, Tosh."

"I am," I say, quick kicking the mute back on. "I mostly am."

"Dude, chill," Cam says. "The guy needs a little break from—"

The sound of glass striking and then shattering recoils through the entire trailer. Devin's music goes dead—I'm not sure how—and the footsteps in the hallway come to a complete stop right outside my door. Seconds tick past as we all just sit and stare at the walls and wait. My pulse revs up with nowhere to go.

"Seven hundred dollars? *For what?*"

The old man lets fly, his voice is so sharp it could split the fake-wood paneling on the walls. When I close my eyes, I can see her face—that look she gets, like she wants to shout back. But she never does. Just lowers her chin, shakes her head small enough so he can barely see, and whispers her thoughts to herself.

Fifteen hundred and eighty-six days of the old man's rage being fueled by her silence.

I adjust the goggles, grip the mouse, click on my max-red stance to boost damage as far as it'll go. It's a calculated risk, I know. I could totally die. It could all be over in seconds. But right now I don't care. Right now I seriously need to kill something, that's all.

"Seven hundred bucks, Amy. That's rent. That's two weeks of groceries."

She says nothing. What could she possibly say to a guy who hasn't worked in almost four years? Who looks at those bills every month like he'll find cheat codes hidden somewhere in all those numbers? Who's so far into this maze, he'll never get out and he knows it? What do you say to a trapped animal? I want to bolt off the chair, go out there, help her find the words, only the last time I did, he let me have it.

There's nothing I can do for her. I'm powerless.

"Two weeks of groceries sittin' useless in that goddamn chair!"

Cam's been bouncing his scrawny ass behind me, just itching to get his hooks on the mouse. But he and Haze stop cold and stare at the bedroom door at the sound of the old man's voice, full of shrapnel and hopelessness.

"Go," Bruiser barks over the headphones, and I turn just in time to catch the platoon plunge onto the once-empty street in the Boneyard.

Mobs swarm toward us, screeching and snapping bug jaws and firing acid spit. One of the healers takes major damage. I shoot the bug that's trying to take her down, watch the metal helmet fly off as it falls over onto its long, flat back, six hairy cockroach legs wiggling in a melodramatic death dance. He's not dead; that's all I know. In a matter of seconds he'll flip over and scurry back to his place in line. They always do—they're roaches. It's almost impossible to kill the damn things. You have to whack 'em multiple times before they'll actually die.

She says something back to him, her muffled voice skulking along the walls of the trailer, too soft to make out the words.

"Like hell," he says. "That son of a bitch pays you minimum wage. And he still charges us to come out and spray!"

Never mind the place is still crawling with roaches. But he doesn't mention that.

My eyes dart away from the screen for a second. I let the echo of his words get distant in my ears, try to tell myself it doesn't matter. Whatever it is, I've either heard it 1,586 times before or I don't want to know. I try to convince myself that the old man's lucky there's a raid going down in the Boneyard, that it's the only thing keeping me in this chair right now. But that's a lie. The truth is, I'm a complete chickenshit when it comes to him. I can't even nut-up enough to protect her.

I adjust the headset over my right ear, pop an earbud into my left, and crank up the volume on both. A couple of clicks on my mp3 player, and Motor City's meld of punk and metal becomes the best raiding soundtrack ever.

Cam leans over my shoulder, breathes wet air next to my ear. "Kill that one!" he says, pointing.

Haze stealth-approaches my closed door, eases his body against it.

The whole house shakes from the impact of my old man's

words on our reality, rattling the thin pane of glass on the windows, until—

Bruiser panic-shouts, cursing over the headset as Six screeches, "Second wave! Second wave!"

A fresh surge of roaches storms over us.

"Shoot those guys!" Cam shouts, leaning way too far into my personal space just so he can point at the screen.

"Dude, back off," I tell him as I click away, giving T-Man an automatic rifle and watching his spread take out six roaches at once. He keeps at it. They're going down, extermination style.

"Buff up!" Bruise calls out over the headset. "Healers, rez the dead now. We've only got seconds."

"Tunnel maps?" I hear over the speaker. I don't recognize the girl's voice. "Need the mapper up front."

"Who are you?" I ask.

"Militiababe," she answers.

Ah. The one from Crazyfire. I think she's a Medic.

We sure as hell could use some heals right about now.

We can't hold out long against numbers like this. The trick is to keep yourself alive, hit the tunnels in the right sequence so you can unlock the last one to the boss before everybody dies. I happen to know how righteously hard it is to stay alive when you're under constant attack, when you can't seem to get the sequence right. We're damn good raiders, but for some reason we can never quite reach that last tunnel. No Ascent Credits. No becoming Worthy. Total fail.

One of these times, it has to end differently.

"I'll map," I say, squaring myself on the seat as I tune out the noise out front.

"Whoa, you're almost to Turk's lair!" Cam shouts. "Yo, T-Man. Assault!"

Haze kicks back over to my bed, tosses his painter's mask in disgust onto a pile of dirty laundry, plops down on the dusty mattress.

"Tosh," he says, his voice a mesh of worry and irritation.

Haze is more of a *see the world, live in the now* kind of guy. He doesn't understand the importance of all this. I've never told him, so of course he wouldn't know. How a fail like me, a guy who can't get it right in real life, would have to roam these maps, to complete these missions. Have to kill the roachlike UnderWorld mobs, rescue the babelike UnderWorld hostages, raid with platoons through the abandoned highways and buildings of the UpperWorld, killing infiltrators and trying to bank Ascent Credits. That's why I bought the new expansion pack. *ASCEND: Armageddon.* It has everything a guy like Caleb Tosh could want in a game: hot chicks, vile insectoid enemies, and the chance to go back and fix whatever I messed up on as long as I don't care how fast I level. If I can nail these missions and get promoted, if I can become Worthy, even an inept guy like me can Ascend a place like the Boneyard.

"Tosh," Haze says again. "Will you get off the game already?"

"He can't!" Cam shrieks. "His platoon is one tunnel away from Turk—the boss, the Cockroach Commandant! Make it happen, T-Man!"

I stare at the tunnels. Twelve of them. My brain whips through all the sequences I've tried in the past. I have a list, only I don't remember where I put it. No time to look, either. The platoon masses behind me, ready to defend, because the second I hit the first tunnel, those cockroach mobs *will* attack.

"Got your back," Militiababe murmurs as she puts herself between T-Man and the platoon. She'll be my healer, but if I don't map fast and shoot straight, she won't last long.

"Ready," Bruise says.

Everybody's green.

Then, quiet as can be, Bruise whispers, "Let's do this."

As I hit Tunnel 6, the mobs shout and pounce.

Everybody starts yelling.

"Where am I supposed to get seven hundred dollars from?"

I tune him out as mobs, both bug and human, charge me. One pops me pretty bad, but Militiababe's on it, healing me as I aim for the next few tunnels, only goddamn it—I just can't get past this one!

Stupid computer. Jesus, why am I so slow?

Oh, right, cuz the old man's a cheap bastard who only springs for the slowest possible Internet connection, then sucks up all the bandwidth himself watching 24-7 crap on our one-and-only TV.

"You're struggling, man," Cam says.

I click like fury. Bars are evaporating to nothing as people crash under the weight of the mobs.

Chinook helicopters roar into view, each bearing the mark of the roach on the side. They fire at the troops below.

"Out of time, T," Bruise yells. "Get it done. Get it effing done, man!"

But I can't. T-Man's losing green like he's bleeding it straight out. Damn!

Outside my room, the old man pushes the volume dial, pierces straight through the chaos of the game.

"What do you mean, he gave you a raise? When did that happen?"

Jesus. I'm dying here. Someone needs to throw some heals, fast.

"What'd you have to do, *sleep with the guy?*"

"At least I'm doing *something.*"

We all stop breathing for a beat, turn toward the door.

Her words nearly flay the skin off my bones. Not her words. Her voice. Out loud, in this house, aimed at him.

Fifteen hundred and eighty-six days now of listening to him rant, and she's *never* talked back to him.

"T-Man!"

I shock-drift back to the screen. Militia's sinking to her knees. She fires one last oh-shit heal at me. I grab the mouse, hulk back up, and bash my way through a cluster of mobs to the last tunnel. *Last one!*

Only, at that exact moment, the stink of truck exhaust drags my attention out the open bedroom window.

I pull down the headset, lean forward, watch in confusion as Stan the Bug Man painstakingly backs his small utility truck down the drive, opens the door, steps out. What the fresh hell? It's Saturday. Stan never works on Saturdays.

The crunch of gravel echoes under Stan's steel-toed boots and the screaming, shattering, twisting whir of full-on cataclysmic assault comes at me right through the headset draped around my neck as I watch Stan approach the house, as I notice there are no canisters or equipment in the back of his truck, as his boots fall flat and hollow on the two wooden steps up to the front door, where he now stands in his gray Dickies even though it's fucking Saturday and I know for sure he's not here to spray.

My face goes numb as flames dot the mini-map on-screen, and battle cries rain down through the headset.

"T-Man!" shouts Militiababe.

Then Bruise. "Where the hell'd you go? We're gonna wipe, man!"

Somebody's swearing in French, and German, too.

I stare through the window at Stan's piss-yellow truck with the four-foot-long fiberglass cockroach perched on top. The stink of my own sweat snaps me out of my daze.

"Stay the hell away from her!" Stan calls out.

Haze gets up off the bed, lifts the tattered curtain aside. "Tosh, man . . . your folks . . ."

The dull throb of ongoing warfare pulses against my chest.

I turn, focus in on the monitor, tighten my gaze on the map. Mortars and machine-gun fire are still exploding up and down the empty highway, the words "The end is near!" keep popping up on-screen all around the dying raiders. No heals or rezzes left. I'm a jump from the tunnel with no green left to give, and there's massive mobs waiting for me.

I have nothing left.

The old man's threats have brought the neighbors to their windows, and my mom . . . my mom screams back this time, for real.

Cam's yelling too, yelling at me to stay in the raid, and I want to, but I keep checking out the window because Stan is loading a bunch of our stuff into his truck: table, chairs, mantel clock, all back where his canisters of poison should be.

"T-Man!" Militiababe calls out. "Get in there. Come on!"

I quick cut my gaze to the Boneyard, the map filling up with a fog so dense, it congeals inside my head.

"Tosh!" Cam barks, reaching for the mouse.

I wave him off, but the shouting out in the front yard rages to new volumes. I lean toward the window, watch as the old man ramrods into Stan, sending him ass over teakettle down the steps. The lamp in his hand shatters into a burgundy mosaic across the walkway, and as he hits the ground, a piece of it jams into the flat of his palm. Blood pumps out fast and wet onto the gravel.

Cam's in front of the computer, freaking out. "Tosh, you can still get to the tunnel, man!"

I turn back just in time to see Bruise die, taken out by a hairy-legged roach mob firing mortar rounds from a truck.

Militiababe's quiet now. She tried to save my stupid ass with good heals, and now I've totally let her down.

"Shit . . ."

"You got her killed," Cam says. "You got them all killed. It's a wipe. Total fail, man."

I throw the headset at Cam without looking, press in next to Haze at the window. Through the sickening yellow tint of the

17

goggles, I watch my mom help Stan to his feet. She's soft with him. Soft in a way she hasn't been with any of us, at least not since the accident.

I catch her eye through the window. The pain on her face hits me like a backhanded blow from the old man.

"What the hell is his problem?" someone shouts over the headset in Cam's hand. "Why isn't he moving?"

Cam lunges at the computer, grabs the mouse. "Tosh! You're still standing. How do I launch? How do I tag the tunnel?"

My mom follows Stan to the truck.

The numbness spreads from my face into my whole entire body.

Something's off. This isn't her typical reboot, like when she gets in her old junker for an hour-long drive around.

Cam's clicking the mouse like crazy. "Jesus, Tosh, this raid isn't over, man."

I drag my gaze from the window to the computer screen, where minion soldiers come spilling out of the tunnels, flooding the abandoned highway. They're everywhere.

Everywhere.

Two truck doors slam shut, one right after the other.

I rip the earbud out of my ear, tear down the hallway, out the door, down the steps. Haze and Cam are on my heels.

"Tosh, wait!"

"Tosh . . . *the game!*"

I run. Fast. Faster than I've ever run before in my entire life. I smell the chemicals leaching out of Stan's truck, the exhaust fumes, four years of dust blowing off our furniture as they drive away.

I can't breathe.

Haze catches up to me first but doesn't say anything. Just stands there watching me watch the truck get smaller and farther away.

Cam is panting by the time he hits my side.

"The Boneyard," he huffs.

I spin around, the street echoing frame by frame through those yellow lenses as I turn.

"Everyone's dead," Cam says, breathless. "The raid's down in flames. Total fucking wipe, man. They'll never take you with them again, Tosh. Never."

He's right.

It's over.

I'm an absolute fail.

− 1.5 −

In the past few weeks alone, I've logged over three hundred hours in the Boneyard.

The goggles really do help.

- 2 -

"Caleb!"

Everything the old man says these days has an exclamation point attached.

He shoves his sweaty, unshaved face into my bedroom.

"I'm goin' down to Goodwill, get us a couch. Watch your brother for me."

Watch my brother for him. Right. Must be a day ending in Y.

He starts to leave, then doubles back.

"There's some boxes in the living room I want you to go through. Keep what you want. Put the rest on the curb."

He leaves my door open, pivoting on the worn-down heel of his boot. I turn back to the game, go back to looking for Militiababe. She's so badass, I want her in my platoon.

"Caleb!"

I jump at the cut of his voice.

"What?"

He's back in my room. Has that dark fog across his face that says he's got rage lurking.

"Get off your ass, get rid of those ridiculous glasses, and go do what I said!"

I wait till I hear the front door slam shut before coming out of my room. The old man's got Devin parked in front of a TV show about hot chicks addicted to venomous snakes.

"He shouldn't be letting you watch that," I say, grabbing the remote. "That's the stupidest premise for a show ever."

Devin rocks back and forth, and I smooth the front of his hair real quick. That always settles him down.

I look around for the boxes the old man mentioned, and through the yellow tint of Cam's gamer specs, I spot them. Three cardboard boxes, stuck halfway behind the TV, all marked TOSS.

My gut tightens. Anything my mom didn't take, the old man's fixing to get rid of. For all I know, he brought some of it with him to Goodwill so he could trade it in on a couch. I slide the boxes toward me as a nervous sweat fogs up the inside of the lenses.

Whatever's in here is all there is.

I push the glasses up since I can't see through the fog anyway, rip the top open on the first one, and start digging my way through the chaos of hair clips; an old apron; a cookbook that once belonged to my grandmother; unopened pack of shoelaces; tubes of half-used lipstick even though I've never seen my mom wear any since the old man thinks it's too fancy; bunch of old rubber bands that are mostly cracked or broken; massive collection of pens and pencils, most dried out and unusable.

And there. At the bottom. A pack of chewing gum.

Except that Amy Tosh doesn't chew gum.

She says the mint makes her stomach sour.

My hands sweat-shake as I lift the flap, as I squeeze the sides to get them to pop out a little, as I pull out the scrap of paper, folded into a small triangle, just like the notes she used to slip into my lunch when I was a kid. *Good luck on your spelling test today, Caleb!*

I turn it over, look at both sides to make sure I'm not missing something on the short, cryptic list.

learn to fly

fly away

Around the edges are a bunch of scrawled, random phrases: *big city, get lucky, regret, somewhere spiritual, sneak in, turn back clock, take me away.*

That's it. No header, no title, no explanation.

I stare at it, wondering what question these words are the answer to. My heart's hitting the side of my rib cage so hard, it feels like something's about to shatter inside me.

Devin starts banging on the tray part of his chair. I look over at him, watch a thread of drool stretch from the corner of his mouth toward his curled-up hand. A hand that used to sock me in the arm just for walking by. That used to muss up my shaggy hair, then smooth down his own perfectly executed side-sweep. That used to fish all the cheese curls out of *my* bag of snack mix, even knowing how bad it would piss me off.

I crawl over to his chair. Collapse next to it. Wrap my arms around the wheel as my gaze drifts unanchored through the room.

My phone buzzes at me from my back pocket. I run my dirty fingernails through my matted hair, pull the phone out, open the app.

The sky will fall and death will beat its wings against the ground.

I'm still tripping over the bizarre text when a gruesome close-up picture of a cockroach comes through.

Shit! I pop it off as hard as I can, watch as it slo-mo fumbles to the ground.

How the hell did a cockroach get into my phone—how does that even happen? Is Commandant Turk menacing me, trying to throw me off the game? Pretty effective strategy, if that's the case.

I try to shake the image out of my head, only now that I've seen it, I can't unsee it. Not the words, not the cockroach picture that came attached—it's all burned into my brain.

I pick up the phone, mash the buttons looking for the photo so I can at least freakin' delete it.

But it's already gone. The cockroach is gone.

Devin bangs harder and louder for his sippy cup. I try to stand, but my legs wobble underneath me, and I can't use my hands because I've got a viselike grip on my phone in one and a viselike grip on my mom's list in the other. I'm crazy-shaking as I cram everything into my pockets, as I stagger to my feet, as I stumble out of the living room.

Only, there in the entryway, I spot Devin's skateboard propped against the wall by the door where it's been leaning, untouched, for the last four years. The breath vapor locks inside me. If I hadn't been such a dick to him that day, he'd be out skating right now, and I'd be giving him shit for his crappy taste in music.

Everything would still be normal.

No wheelchair.

No fifteen hundred and eighty-seven fights.

No bug truck, hauling her out of here like a piece of used furniture.

My whole life, reset back to default mode.

By the time I reach the kitchen, the tears are shudder-sobbing through every hollow inch of my body.

I fumble in the dark for the light switch, hit it.

The wallpaper goes supernova.

Cockroaches.

Everywhere.

They're shooting out of the cracks in the walls, out of holes in the windowsills, out of rips in the wallpaper. I try to rake them out of my hair, scratch them out from under my skin, but they keep coming and coming, amassing along the empty highway, blockading the entrance to the tunnels. Every single one of them is scatting out the words "the end is here," just like that day in the Boneyard. Only this time, it's *my* survival bar that's depleting.

The chirr of trillions of roaches floods my ears, and I throw my arms over my head to block out the sound as I sink to the floor.

- 2.5 -

Militiababe wore an odd kind of mask that covered the lower half of her face but not her eyes. You'd think that would make it easier to find her. Not in reality, of course. In reality, Militiababe could look like pretty much anything.

But I'm still hoping to come across her again in-game.

A girl in a half mask can't just disappear. Can she?

- 3 -

A shard of blistering sunlight hits me straight through my closed eyelids.

I wake up groggy, all crust and confusion, with no memory of what happened last night. Did the old man put me to bed? I'm usually the one who takes care of *him* at night. That's the ritual: brush my teeth, put on my least-dirty T-shirt, scoop up the dozen or so empties from around the couch, and leave a light on in the kitchen so he doesn't break his fucking neck in case he decides at some point to get up and go to his room.

I roll over, still hazy, pick some of the junk out of my eyes, get them to focus just in time to see the cockroach scurry across my pillow.

I hit the wall in a flash.

My gaze ricochets uncontrollably around the room until I spot the computer on. The Boneyard's up and running even though I always make sure the Relic gets shut down at night. I squint at the screen, at the highway map teeming with UnderWorld mobs, turn back to the cockroach on my pillow that's waving its antennae at me like a middle finger.

I don't know how he found me, or how he got into my room from the Boneyard. But I have to kill him. I have to get him and kill him before he brings the rest of Turk's army back here and all hell breaks loose.

I scramble back to the bed, flick the little bastard onto the floor. Its hairy legs flail in the air for a second or two before it flips over and beelines up the wall. I quick grab a sneaker and start smashing the holy hell out of it for two full minutes. The crunching exoskeleton makes my stomach roil, but I ignore it. You have to go full tilt to kill a cockroach. They're virtually indestructible, and I want this one ten kinds of dead.

I grunt and swing and finally my arm falls limp at my sides while I stand there panting. The roach is nothing more than a splotch of brown pigment and yellow gut paint now, and I sink to my knees, fighting to catch my breath. I use a dirty sock off the floor to wipe sweat and tears and snot from my face.

My red-rimmed gaze drifts over to the door, and suddenly it hits me.

All that pounding.

All that smashing against the foam-board walls of this trailer . . . and the old man hasn't come in to yell at me for it.

I stumble out of my bedroom in a daze, down the hall, into the living room, where the TV's on but no one's watching it. I stop, blink in disbelief around the empty room, at the spot on the couch where the old man should be parked in front of the TV but isn't.

Waves of blue-gray light pulse at me from the mute screen, and I take one guarded step after another toward it, kneel gape-mouthed on the floor. The events unfolding on-screen slowly register in my head, and before I know it, the trailer feels like it's missing a wheel, like everything's slanting to one side.

I grab the remote off the TV table, unmute it, change the channel again and again, but every station it's the same thing. Even the sports and cooking shows have crawlers across the bottom.

MASSIVE BIRD DIE-OFF IN OHIO. EXPERTS BAFFLED.

I tumble backward, sink onto the floor, keep watching, listening.

"Scientists are baffled by a massive bird die-off discovered early this morning at an amusement park in Sandusky, Ohio." The anchorwoman smiles as she says it. There's something absolutely skeletal about her toothy grin.

The shot cuts over to video footage taken down at Goofy Golf. The mini-golf course, the go-kart track, even the bumper-boat pool, all littered with bird carcasses.

The remote trembles in my hand as the video switches to an interview with some world-renowned bird expert.

"We're looking into the possibility of an electrical storm that passed over Ohio last night as being a plausible source of the die-off," the man says. "But frankly, at the moment, we're just not sure."

The feed cuts back to the footage of the dead birds as the field reporter blathers on. But something catches my eye, and it catches the cameraman's eye, too, because he focuses right in on the bright green drink cup lying on the track in the middle of all that black carnage. The shot gets tighter and tighter until he's right on top of it, and I'm barely breathing as I listen to the anchorwoman declare that the birds all died in flight, that their dead bodies literally fell out of the sky.

But not this one. This one's still alive, just barely, but alive and struggling to flap its wings against the ground like it's begging for someone to notice it isn't dead.

The sky will fall and death will beat its wings against the ground.

Synapses start firing and misfiring in my brain; incoherent thoughts, truths, half-truths, and flat-out lies, all going at it simultaneously.

This can't be the same bird that dive-bombed me and Haze on my twelfth birthday. . . .

That bird is dead. We killed it. We didn't mean to. It just happened.

So why is it still alive? I mean, here it is on the TV screen, next to the green cup Haze threw onto the track that day, and it's alive, and it's begging to be saved.

I spin my gaze around the trailer again, chill bumps running up my arms. Where the hell's the old man, seriously? He should be sitting here right now, scratching his well-developed pony keg through the decaying fabric of his shirt, spewing conspiracy theories at the TV.

I fall forward again, crawl toward the screen for a better view, only my cell phone slips off my lap and vibrates a text alert at me.

I do the slow-motion-reach thing, pick it up off the floor, tap it open.

It's the cockroach. The goddamn cockroach, the one I just killed in my room. That motherfucker is tracking me.

The end is near, it says.

I panic, ratchet my arm back, hurl the phone against the wall, hear the sickening crack of plastic and glass against wall board.

"Text me now, you bastard!" I yell, only I know Turk can't hear me—for one thing, because I think I just busted the shit out of my phone, and for another, if I'd actually ever found Commandant Turk, I would have Ascended by now.

My heart sinks straight through the bottom of the trailer.

The end is near.

Jesus, that's what it said on the map during the raid that day. All those platoons, fleeing the tunnels in flames, every one of them tagged with the same line of words where it should've been nothing but green.

I panic-scan the room.

Where are they?

I scramble to my feet, fly down the hallway, kick open Devin's bedroom door.

Empty.

The old man's, too.

The car's not in the drive.

Ragged breath shreds through my lungs. It's not like that

coward to just go off, especially not with Devin. He never takes Devin.

Unless there was some kind of emergency.

I clamp my eyes shut against the far-distant sound of sirens, the cries for help, the helicopter blades that airlifted Devin off the track at Goofy Golf that day.

The end is near. Shit. Who would send a message like that?

I retrieve my phone, carefully slide the cover back to reveal a massively cracked screen. The way I threw it, I'm shocked it's not dead. But it isn't—it even buzzes in my hand as I reread that last text through the cracked screen.

I quick open the new message, terrified it's the old man about to lay some kind of gut-wrenching, nut-filled turd on me.

It's not.

It's a text. I don't know from who, exactly, only that the two-word message hits my brain like a mortar round.

Save it.

I stagger back down the hall toward the living room, hoping to see the old man sitting there, hoping against hope that my brother's with him, that they're watching *Roundhouse*, or even *Promzillas*, and drinking beer and eating the bag of snack mix I hid in the back of the cupboard for safekeeping.

Anything but knowing he went off and left me here alone in this roach-infested trailer.

I catch a glimpse of Devin's skateboard in the entryway and stop short. Take a sharp turn, pick it up, run my fingers across the sandpaper finish, over the Mexican Virgin Mary painted on the bottom. I never asked him why he picked a deck that had a religious symbol on it; I mean, we're not even Mexican, let alone Catholic. Now, thanks to that bird, I'll never know.

The low sound of the news broadcast drifts through the trailer like dust particles, and I angle my face toward the TV.

They're still sucking every ounce of lifeblood out of the dead-bird story.

For the umpteenth time, they replay the clip with the green drink cup and the barely alive bird next to it, and it hits me.

I bet that's where the old man went.

I bet in his twisted logic, he figured he'd take my brother down there to see the birds, not thinking that the last time any of us went to Goofy Golf was the day I practically killed Devin. Besides, the old man has no idea that me and Haze committed birdicide that day, but I do. And somewhere, buried deep in his mostly abandoned head, Devin knows it too.

Save it.

The bird. I wonder if I'd get Ascent Credits for saving that bird, for getting that one thing right this time.

Adrenaline speeds through me as I toggle my gaze between the TV and the skateboard, and before I can give it a rational dose of thought, I throw the front door open, deck in hand. *I'll bring it right back,* I silently promise Devin.

But as my foot hits the top step, the echo of Stan's work boot ripples the thick air around me. I glance up, half expecting his Termi-Pest truck to be backed into the driveway, even though I know it's impossible. That truck, Stan, my mom, they're long gone.

I palm the side of my head to knock the thought out of it, to kill the noise. I pop in an earbud, quick scroll through my music files, fire up a little Bunny Puke, and bump up the volume as high as I can stand it.

Halfway down the block, I toss the skateboard onto the ground and hop on. It isn't long before I remember what an incompetent skater I am and what a gigantic dickweed I must look like, thrash-spasming just to stay upright. But I elbow my deflating ego to the side just for the moment because I need to find that bird. Somehow I'm supposed to save it—the message said so.

Not that it matters about my lack of boarding skills since there's no one out here to impress. Not a soul on the streets. No cars, no pedestrians. I might as well be skating down an abandoned highway in the Boneyard.

My heart is moshing against my ribs as I whiffle into the parking lot of Goofy Golf and stumble off the skateboard.

A mind-boggling number of news vans have lined up end-to-end along the frontage to the park. Some of the vans are from Ohio stations, but most of them sport out-of-state call letters painted on the sides, and all of them have satellite erections springing out of some unseen orifice in the vehicles' roofs. The parking lot is littered with talking heads and cameras and microphones, and in the middle of it all, one lone, bright yellow truck that looks suspiciously like Stan's bug-mobile, right down to the oversized cockroach on top. The sight of it trips a hate-wire inside me, but I can't let myself stumble over that—not now.

I hop off Devin's deck, pocket my earbuds and phone, and take a view of my surroundings. I'm grateful to be on solid ground, but I can't deny the severe muscle throb from the shock of physical activity as I make my way unnoticed through the maze of cars and cables and journalists.

I struggle to orient myself in the midst of all the chaos. The spin in my head, the ring in my ears . . . the overwhelming sense of being knocked off-balance. I force myself to focus, to remember that the reporter had been standing down in the go-kart pit. So I need to shake it off, because my first order of business is to find that discarded drink cup with the bird next to it.

If I didn't know this place so well, I'd have to start randomly walking around looking for it. But that won't be necessary. Because just a few feet from the reporter was a skid mark up on the wall at a sharp curve on the track, and the discarded drink cup was on the ground below it. I know that part of the track all too well.

Me and Haze were the ones who made that skid mark.

I spit the thought out onto the sidewalk and look around through the yellow-tinged goggles.

No wonder the streets of Sandusky are empty—the park is mobbed with people. I'm getting a definite preraid Boneyard vibe here.

Unfortunately, with crowds like these, I stand a pretty slim chance that anyone's going to let me down onto the track.

If I'd have thought this through for even one second, I would have realized that I needed a more elaborate plan than stealing my brother's Virgin Mary skateboard and rolling up to an amusement park full of people who aren't going to want me here, then trying to find a skid mark and a cup so I can save a dying little bird on the advice of some mystery texter who may or may not be an UpperWorld operative trying to save me from the infestation of Turk's army that started in my room this morning.

But I didn't think it through for more than one second, so that's all I've got.

For a few seconds I contemplate what Roundhouse would do.

In a moment such as this, when TV's Chuck Norris–inspired Roundhouse finds himself in an impossible situation and has to figure his way out with nothing but brains, brawn, and his own saliva, I have reason to believe that he would create a distraction of some kind. He would do so by pulling a Chinese firecracker out of his ass, or fashioning his own hair into a smoke bomb, and as the crowd swarmed to see if they were under terrorist attack or something, Roundhouse would dash in, do his business, and get out before anyone knew he'd been there.

Unfortunately, I don't know how to fashion a smoke bomb out of my own hair.

I need to come up with a plan B.

I survey the amusement-park grounds, the castle that's the hallmark of the mini-golf course, not to mention the place where Logan Ward claims to have lost his virginity to Sabrina Jones last summer. Past that, there's the serpentine pit of the go-kart track, the bumper-boat pond filled with dead birds and disembodied black feathers floating around in it, plus the inevitability of infectious diseases and the budding stench of death. I'm not exaggerating; just check out the way the entire place is swarming with people in hazmat suits.

Wait a minute. Wait. A. Minute. *That's it.*

Plan B involves Caleb Tosh in a hazmat suit.

How legit is *that?*

- 3.5 -

So far, there are no signs of UnderWorld infiltration.

I breathe a sigh of relief.

- 4 -

The question is, what kind of dumb-ass hazmat team leaves the back doors of their van open?

Doesn't matter, because here I stand at the back of the van, and there, just inside the open doors, is a stack of white, disposable Tyvek coveralls. Another quick check reveals a box of disposable face masks just behind the suits. This stroke of luck has me a little freaked out, since I don't have the most stellar reputation for being lucky.

But I'll take it.

I've never moved faster in my life to accomplish any goal than I move now, gearing up in that Tyvek suit. Once I'm dressed, I make my way toward the park, only to realize I have one more little snag: Devin's skateboard. Hazmat dudes generally don't carry their skateboards with them.

I hear a faint *tick-tick-ticking* in my head, like if I don't find that bird and save it fast, this whole level will wipe again and I'll lose everything. I quick stash the deck inside the back of that yellow truck parked nearby, only because it'll be easier to find in the sea of white vans when I'm done here. Besides, I know it's not Stan's truck. Stan's truck didn't have any equipment in the back the last time I saw it.

I fake stride across the entrance to the park, very authoritative and official-like, still mystified that no one so much as does a double take in my direction.

I take that back. A girl in black Chuck Taylors and a SUPERGIRL T-shirt leans over the chain-link fence. There's nothing noteworthy about her, except that she's the only one who seems to be tracking my entrance. I hop down the stairs two at a time, head to the go-kart pit, pick up the pace until I'm around the first bend, and only then do I break into a jog-walk toward the discarded cup near the skid mark, which I know is somewhere around the third turn. The ground is littered with festering bird carcasses. It's a grotesque enough sight by itself, but I have to dodge them as I go, like some creepy, morbid version of Frogger.

My hyperventilating breath pools inside the toxic-smelling mask until I start to feel claustrophobic, and the more I focus on the claustrophobia, the more I start to panic, which makes me totally question the whole point of coming here; and just as I'm about to give up, to ditch the hazmat suit and the mask, retrieve the skateboard from where I stashed it in the bug truck, and thrash-spasm my way back home, there it is.

The skid mark.

The cup.

And the bird. Still alive, still trying to flap its little wings against the pavement.

Alive. But barely.

I squat down, look into its little black BB of an eyeball, hoping it'll offer me some kind of insight of greater meaning. It doesn't. It just stares back, pleading.

I pull the toxic paper mask down over my chin, suck in a couple lungfuls of fresh air over my shoulder, blink tears off the surface of my eyes. *Save it*, the message said.

I'm trying, I swear.

I run my hands over the front of the hazmat suit, find a pocket with a pair of latex gloves tucked inside. I put them on, lean over, pick up the green drink cup, and scoop the bird inside even though it takes me a couple of passes because I can't get my hands to stop shaking like crazy. I'm careful to put the little guy in feet first so it can breathe and not feel claustrophobic, the way I felt a moment ago inside this paper mask.

I hold the cup up to eye level, stare into the bird's unblinking little face, and smile for the first time in weeks.

We did it, I convey telepathically. *You made it—I saved you. Looks like I'll get to level after all.*

I keep looking, though, keep looking as if the bird is going to open its beak and thank me or something. But it doesn't. Within seconds, it stops pulsing its exhausted wings against the insides of the cup, and I hold my breath, waiting for it to restart. But it never does.

It's dead.

The bird is dead.

The go-kart track starts to bend and stretch around me and I'm sure I'm going to black out, only my phone starts buzzing in my back pocket just then. I reach to answer it, but it's buried under a layer of Tyvek so super-constructed that there's no way to rip through it. I have to unzip, reach around, fish it out with one hand while holding a dead, probably disease-infested bird in a used drink cup with the other.

I finally get the phone out.

It's the cockroach. Grotesquely cracked and fragmented in my broken screen.

What the fuck, man?

The cockroach found me.

My arm drops as I spin one way, then the other, looking for signs of an onslaught I know must be coming. But there's nothing. No one. Not even backup to keep *my* sorry ass out of hot water. I'm alone, all alone on the go-kart track at Goofy Golf with a dead bird in one hand and a dead phone in the other.

Helicopter blades pulse through the air somewhere off in the distance, and the mantel clock Stan threw in the back of his truck *tick-tick-ticks* from an unseen place behind me, followed by the synchronized cadence of marching feet, which can mean only one thing.

Jesus. I had one job: save the bird and collect the Ascent Credits so I could become Worthy. Well, I blew it. And now I probably just wiped. Again.

I'm seriously gonna need some backup if I have any hope of getting out of here. My fingers mash the buttons on the phone, frantically dialing numbers—first Cam, who doesn't answer, then Napoleon Burger since Haze doesn't have a cell phone.

"Come on," I urge, bouncing with nerves inside my hazmat suit. "Come on, answer!"

The mechanical click-and-report behind me sends echoes of terror through my entire body.

My hand falls slowly away from the side of my head as I lift my gaze equally slowly up the sides of the go-kart pit.

Holy mother of—

I'm half expecting to see news cameras stationed around the perimeter of the track because of all the vans out front. Instead I find myself surrounded by a wall of weps—I don't know whose, but there must be dozens of them, staked out along both sides of the pit, aimed straight at me.

I lift my hands skyward—I've run through maps like this enough times to know how it works.

"Drop the cup!" one of the soldiers yells from behind me.

I do. I let it fall from my fingers, consumed by a sickness I can't reconcile as the carcass of that recently deceased bird bounces partway out onto the concrete track. *I'm sorry*, I whisper to the bird, but it sends nothing back.

"Now the phone!" the voice behind me shouts.

My alarms go off. No way am I dropping my phone onto the concrete track on purpose. It won't survive another violent mishap.

"Drop the phone!"

I crouch down, place it gently on the ground next to the cup.

My eye catches the sight of the bird's little wing draped lightly over the rim, and I swallow against the slow burn in my throat. Damn bird. I was supposed to save it. I made it here in time and everything. Why'd it have to wait till I showed up to go and die?

"Turn around nice and slow," the voice behind me orders.

I rotate a hundred and eighty degrees, only to find myself staring down the barrel of at least a dozen different kinds of weapons, and it hits me.

I don't think I'm in Kansas anymore.

- 5 -

"**You don't understand,**" I tell the odd collection of soldier dudes for the fortieth time. "I don't *work* for anyone. I'm not *affiliated* with any organization. I'm a just a high school kid. I don't even get good grades."

They huddle-whisper after every statement I make, their voices low enough where I can't even tell what language they're speaking. The matching bowl-cut hairdos, the strange but identical camo-style fatigues, the weps that don't look like anything we've been using in the Boneyard (although admittedly I haven't unlocked everything from the expansion pack yet). Still, nothing about this has any ring of familiarity to it. I have no idea what I'm dealing with here.

All I know is, I was supposed to save that bird and I failed. I didn't get to call for backup when I was standing on the go-kart track at Goofy Golf. I let my brigade down on this mission.

Couldn't even keep Turk from infiltrating my phone afterward.

Wait.

"Where's my phone?" I ask in a panic.

"In for analysis," one of the men says.

Analysis?

"What about my wallet?"

"In for analysis."

"And my skateboard?"

The commando shoots me a lethal glance before saying, "In for analysis." I finish the sentence with him, and for a split second his eyes glow an enraged, biohazard green.

I sneak a look around as the group of soldiers reconvenes. The room looks vaguely familiar. Opaque brick walls made of some kind of composite material and a few acrylic chairs surround a single backlit, acrylic table. That's it. Just me in a room full of virtually invisible furniture with a bunch of guys who look like extras from every B-grade sci-fi movie ever made.

"Why am I here?" I say, raising my voice. "I didn't do anything wrong."

In-for-analysis pushes right up against me, and the idea pops over my head like a burst thought bubble. Of course I did something wrong. I probably committed a whole convoy of wrongs at Goofy Golf alone. Not that I'd tell *him* that. Confess nothing—that'll be my motto.

"Look," a second commando says, circling around, closing in on me nice and tight. "I don't think you appreciate the seriousness of the situation."

I'm flanked at this point—I have no choice but to agree. I swallow against the dry panic in my mouth.

"Maybe I don't."

"You trespassed onto a crime-scene investigation."

"Are you guys CSI—is that what you're saying?"

He ignores me, continues down the litany of my offenses.

"You broke into a municipal vehicle, stole government property." He leans forward. "You impersonated a hazmat officer."

"So you're Feds?"

His fist comes down hard on the table. *Who do you work for?*

I refuse to show him I'm intimidated.

"Why should I tell you who I work for when you won't even tell me who you are?"

A third commando pulls his chair up in front of me and straddles it backward. He doesn't lean close, doesn't crowd me with aggressive energy. He crosses his arms over the back of the chair and drops his voice to a whisper so low that *I'm* the one who has to lean in.

"Just tell us what you were doing," he says, keeping his voice calm and low, "and we can clear this whole thing up right here, right now."

My gaze boomerangs between them. If I say what really happened, they might kill me. If I don't, they'll probably for sure kill me. I realize with dire certainty that I have to come up with something to say that won't culminate in them wanting me dead.

"Look, if I tell you what I was doing, you'll legitimately think I'm a wuss," I tell the guy.

"No, I won't." He leans over, drilling into me with his commando-vision. "I'll think you're a goddamn hero."

I swallow hard, look around at the commandos. What's in it for me if I comply? Level jumps? Special weps? Extra rezzes? I'd give anything for the chance to finally get this shit right. Still, something tells me it's in my best interest to be only partly truthful.

"Okay, well, I was watching the news this morning." I pause for dramatic effect. Even a lie sounds more believable if you whisper it. "And I saw a bird lying on the go-kart track. And I noticed it wasn't dead like all those other birds." I skip the part about the message on my phone, study the circle of pinched faces around me. "I decided to come down and save it."

The commando doesn't move, doesn't budge, doesn't so much as twitch for one full minute. Then he scrapes his chair back so suddenly I just about disintegrate inside my own skin. He circles up the wagons, and they confer again behind me.

I sneak glances at the mottled gray-purple-black of their huddled uniforms, wishing I could hear what they're saying. Unfortunately, these guys, whoever they are, have perfected the art of the stealth-whisper.

The third commando breaks free of the group, comes back, and sits across from me again.

"Caleb Tosh," he says in a dark hush. "Are you familiar with Turk's army?"

He can't be serious.

"Why?" I ask.

"You're aware of the upcoming battle?"

He notes my skepticism.

"You've seen them, haven't you?" He says it so quietly, I can barely hear him. "Scouts? Infiltrators?"

I try not to let him see me gulp. "Yes."

"We believe you can be of service to us."

I'm blinking like a crazy person behind the yellow goggles, but I can't stop myself from asking, "What are you talking about?"

"It will require an extreme level of internal fortitude," he continues in a whisper, every word coming faster. "You will see things. *Strange* things."

"Stranger than five thousand dead birds in an amusement park?" I say.

He ignores me. "And you will be asked to do things that may not seem to follow typical mission protocol. You must not question the mission."

"What's the catch?" I ask.

"We know where Turk's lair is. And it's not what you think."

My ears start to ring. What he's suggesting . . . well, it's impossible. "Then, wh—"

The other soldiers move in fast, form a semicircle around us. Commando Number Three pulls back, raises his voice to mid-volume. "You're free to go," he says.

Wait, *what?*

"But you said—"

"I said. You are free. To go." His expression turns hard, matching his cohorts'.

"Oh. Okay." I look around, not sure what to do next. "So . . . can I have my stuff back?"

"It will remain in custody until we've completed our analysis," the first guy says.

"But you're welcome to take this," one of the others tells me, handing me a plastic ziplock baggie with the now-dead bird inside. "Give it a proper burial."

I reel with disgust.

"Don't you need *this* for analysis?" I ask, unable to keep the sarcastic twinge out of my voice. I can't even look at the bird as I pinch the baggie between the tips of two fingers. Bastards confiscated the gloves along with my Tyvek suit and the rest of my stuff.

"Thousands more where that came from," he says.

But this one made it out alive.

Until it had to go and die.

As I reach the door, I turn, eye the commandos one last time. They've gone on with their business, ignoring me so completely, it's almost like I was never there to begin with.

I head outside with nothing to show for my trouble but a dead bird in a ziplock bag. The little black carcass bobs up and down in time with my footsteps, like it's still trying to flap its lifeless wings.

Save it.

I hang my head as I walk home. Serves me right to go off on a mission without a platoon. I wouldn't even blame them if I got stripped of my rankings. They already threatened to leave me behind for good once before; I had to do a humiliating amount of groveling to get back in. Jesus, I don't know what I'd do if I got left in the Boneyard alone.

Plus, now the old man's going to kill me for losing my phone.

But not before I kill myself for letting them keep Devin's skateboard after promising him I'd bring it right back.

My guts are in a complete twist by the time I pass the mailbox in front of my house. It's halfway open; inside is a fat envelope with my name on it.

I quick drop the baggie to the ground, pull out the contents of the envelope: my cell phone, my wallet, and the now-crushed drink cup.

The empty manila envelope flutters from my hands, lands in the dirt next to the ziplock bird. Nothing's missing from my wallet; even the screen on the phone looks brand-spanking-new. Baffled, I flip it over, unlock the screen, check my settings—this is definitely my phone; it's all here. Nothing's been changed or deleted—just mysteriously repaired.

Did those commandos do me a solid and fix my phone to prove they're legit? Note to self: check my Trade Screen next time I log into the Boneyard.

Meanwhile, I do a panoramic sweep of the street. Nothing suspicious jumps out—no unmarked cars with blacked-out windows, no strange pedestrians trying to appear incognito as they scurry down the sidewalk. In fact, there doesn't seem to be a living soul around.

Devin.

The old man.

I never saw them at Goofy Golf.

I take the two wooden steps to the trailer in one leap, turn the handle, stop dead in my tracks.

Devin's skateboard is parked right inside the door like it always is. I flip it over, check for the scuffed-up Virgin Mary on the bottom.

She's there.

I slide my gaze toward the living room, half expecting to see one of those commandos sitting there next to the old man, catching an episode of *Promzillas* with a beer in one hand and a powdered doughnut in the other. But the only signs of life inside the trailer come from the TV—still on, still throbbing gray-blue light into the room.

This has got to be some kind of nacho-and-Mountain Dew–induced hallucination.

I hear a muffled commotion coming from down the hall, picture Devin, tipped over in his chair, lying helpless on the floor while I've been dicking around on a pointless mission down at Goofy Golf. I sprint to his room, but it's empty; then head for mine, throw my shoulder into the door.

It's not Devin.

It's the Relic. Turned on, logged in, already in play.

I taste stale air through my open mouth as I approach the desk, as I lower myself one vertebra at a time onto the squeaky chair. My toon is lurking, watching a group of raiders who have found a way UnderGround. I can't tell if it's one of the tunnels they're wandering around in or somewhere else; I'm not even sure if this is a legitimate platoon or some kind of trap. All I know is the subterranean walls are made of opaque bricks—like the interrogation room I was just in.

I square the gaming glasses on my face, promise myself I'll just hang back, that I'm not going to join. Haze thinks I'll lose myself in the game, and I made him a promise to stop; but following a group just to watch what they're up to isn't the same as playing. At least that's how I get it to work out in my head.

The tunnel raiders look a little unsure of themselves, almost like wherever they are, they're surprised to be there. Or scared. They make slow, awkward advances through the maze of tunnels, their hybrid penlight-wands not nearly bright enough for them to see what's coming. Probably why it looks like they're just fumbling around in the dark.

I'd send my toon back to the surface to try to find the rest of my platoon, but I don't exactly know where I am. The mini-map on-screen is oddly pixilated, like the Relic is having an aneurysm or something, so even that's no help.

There's a kind of weight to being isolated and alone. It's starting to crack me a little.

I hop off the chair, poke my head out the bedroom door, hoping to catch the old man coming back from getting fried chicken or whatever else would be enough of an incentive to get him to leave the house with Devin.

Still nothing.

I stand in the doorway of my room like I'm in Boneyard limbo, halfway between the UnderWorld and the UpperWorld—half waiting for the old man and Devin to turn up again and half watching the action on-screen play out like a Three Stooges routine. T-Man is hiding in a little alcove as the raiders start scattering, bumping into each other, darting off in different directions, barking orders on chat with no clear leadership. I wipe my sweaty palms against the grunge-funk of my pant legs just to stop myself from running over and grabbing the mouse. *It's not my platoon*, I remind myself. *It could be a trap.*

My gaze clicks back and forth from the living room to the computer screen, watching for movement, for anything that will start making sense either here or in the Boneyard.

And then—

Three guys break loose from the brigade. They're wearing mottled gray-purple-black fatigues, their bowl-cut hair flapping behind them as they dash past me through the opaque tunnel and around a set of turns. Once they've lost the others, one of them takes his penlight-wand device and taps out a pattern on the bricks, and I swear on the Scrolls of Turk that a secret passageway opens up right there. I rush to the computer, grab the mouse, follow as the soldiers hurry down a narrow hidden staircase. The last one turns his head before he disappears into the passageway, shoots a look straight at T-Man, and gives a single nod.

T-Man stays on their heels up the stairway and through a tunnel opening, spilling out onto a completely different highway. A fat yellow car is already running, waiting, puffing exhaust straight at my toon until he's swallowed by dense gray smog. The commandos look around, hop in the car, and take off.

The slam of the front door rocks me like a five-hundred-volt shock.

I dart into the hallway, but it's not the old man and Devin coming toward me.

It's Haze.

My gaze drops to the manila envelope in his hand, the crushed green drink cup, the ziplock bag with the dead bird inside.

"I found this stuff out front," he says. "Thought you'd want it."

I don't want it. I wish I'd never seen it. Any of it.

"So what's—" He stops short, locks on to the computer screen. "Tosh."

"I'm not playing," I tell him.

"The hell."

If I weren't so supremely grateful to see another human being at this point, I'd kick his ass for constantly riding mine about the game.

Haze holds the bird carcass out to me.

"What's this about?" he asks.

"Souvenir."

"What are *you* doing with it?"

"I'm supposed to bury it."

My insides scream blood and fire, leeching molten sweat out of every inch of my skin.

I wasn't supposed to bury it. I was supposed to save it. That was the mission. I already killed that bird once, on my twelfth birthday, and it was the catalyst, man, the catalyst for everything. And here I am—I mean, I bought the expansion pack and it gave me a second chance to nail the mission, to earn my Ascent Credits by saving the bird, only I'm such an ass-nugget, I blew that, too. What a fail.

Unless . . .

Unless giving it a proper burial is the way in. That's what the commandos told me to do.

The baggie dangles from Haze's fingers as the buzz of an incoming text message derails my train of thought.

"You gonna get that?" he says.

I'm jackhammering. I take out the phone, tap the mysteriously resurrected screen, brace for the cockroach picture I'm sure will be there.

But it's not.

It's a plain text, no image.

You will see things.

"Tosh?"

I follow my own line of vision back to the Relic, to the Boneyard. My toon has hitched a ride with the three commandos who have parked the yellow car in a wooded area and are digging a hole in the ground. One of them throws something into the pit, and even though I can't see what it is, I know.

Okay, so I bury the bird, so what? Do I get my Ascent Credits? Do I level at that point?

Not to mention, the commando who said I could be of service to them did an abrupt about-face two seconds later. So I hope they can understand my skepticism regarding this quasi-message they're showing me from the Boneyard.

You must not question the mission.

"Tosh—"

The catch in Haze's voice grabs me. I turn, see the way he's eyeing me . . . like I'm—

"I don't care what you say, man. I'm not crazy." I push the goggles up off my face because they're too sweat-fogged to see through.

He makes a face but doesn't answer. In fact, neither of us says anything for a while. He comes over, sits on my bed, starts fiddling with the gizmos on his mask while I fake key the words "save it" over and over again on my phone.

"I never said you were crazy," he says at last. "It's just—I'm—you know. The game."

"I already told you, I don't play anymore. I just like to tune in sometimes and see what's going on."

"I'm not an idiot, Tosh. Just because I don't play doesn't mean I don't know how it works. It doesn't work like that."

"It helps sometimes, that's all."

He opens his mouth like he's going to argue the point, but he doesn't. Instead he shuts up again and nods his head, just one time.

I close my eyes for a quick second against a twinge of déjà vu. My mom did that nod thing all the time. The old man would be raging as Dev and I cowered in a corner, terrified, and she'd look at us without saying a word and nod just like that. Just once. Like it would all be okay somehow.

My red-rimmed eyes gravitate back to the Boneyard, to the yellow car with the black-and-white checkerboard around the top, wheezing in front of a row of rangy trees.

"So," Haze says, holding up the bird. "You want help burying this?"

My attention drifts from the monitor back to Haze.

"You'll do anything to keep me out of the Boneyard, won't you?"

He smiles, adjusts his knit cap, tosses the baggie at me. I catch it in a tight grip so it doesn't slip out of my hands, offer the bird a silent apology in case I hurt it by grabbing too hard.

Out back the old man's got an overgrown junk heap, but I can't find anything useful enough to dig a hole with. Just old tuna cans, a rust-covered slotted spoon—nothing that'll dig deep enough or fast enough to get this over with and make the whole bird thing go away.

I know we have a long-forgotten shovel around here somewhere.

I eventually find it camouflaged in a pile of rotting lumber.

Haze holds the bird while I start digging. I don't talk, just kick out shovelfuls of dirt. It would be accurate to say that Haze is less of a stranger to physical labor than I am, but this one's on me. Still, I'm a panting, sweat-spewing mess before I've managed to dig anything deep enough to bury a bug in, let alone a bird.

I don't understand why it had to go and die. I mean, it must have known that someone was coming to save it; otherwise, why would it have fought so hard? What good does it do to stay alive through all the crap stuff only to give up right at the end, just when things are about to turn around?

The sky will fall and death will beat its wings against the ground.

They called it. Whoever sent me that message totally called

it. Was it the commandos? Did they intentionally lure me to Goofy Golf so I'd get back on this map? For all I know, the interrogation they put me through earned me Ascent Credits. It freakin' should have.

"Yo, Tosh," Haze says. "That's probably deep enough."

I look down at the two-foot hole I dug without realizing it, pull my arm across my face to wick away the sweat, only to find a big line of snot across my sleeve.

Luckily, Haze doesn't point out that I'm standing here crying over a dead bird in a plastic bag.

"What are you going to bury it in?" he asks instead.

"What do you mean?"

"Well, you can't just throw it in the ground. That's kind of disrespectful."

"How is that disrespectful?"

"It was a living thing, Tosh," he says. Like I need to be reminded. "It deserves a proper burial."

"It's in a bag," I say.

"It won't be able to decay like that."

The word eats through my body—I close my eyes against the unexpected sensation of the ground shifting from solid to semisolid.

"Look," Haze says, "just bury it in this."

He hands me the crushed drink cup. As it passes from his hand to mine, I hear the roar of go-karts off in the distance, feel the thrill of freedom as he and I scramble into the bucket seats, hear him slurp the tail end of a soda, watch the cup arc in slow motion onto the track just as we accelerate.

My mom begged the old man not to have my party there. She said she had a bad feeling.

I take the cup, turn it over in my fingers, force my eyes to unblur so I can read the words.

Subway. City Hall Station.

. . . the note. My mom's note.

big city

Yeah. Big city.

Where the City Hall Station's located.

Which is probably a subway entrance.

Subways go underground.

UnderGround. UnderWorld.

The mission starts to come into focus right before my eyes.

This is exactly why I got the expansion pack. Thanks to *ASCEND: Armageddon*, I can go back, fix my biggest mistake. Sure, it'll take me longer to level, but if it keeps me from letting Stan take my mom, it'll be worth it.

I can do that. I can find my way UnderGround, now that I understand how to get there. I've already made it to that map enough times. I can start this rogue mission without my platoon. No doubt they'll join me once they see how close I am to finding Turk, to killing the shit out of him, to becoming Worthy.

The phone buzzes in my pocket. I throw down the shovel, pull up the message.

The world beneath will weep blood.

Whoa . . .

It's all coming together.

The commandos didn't jack that yellow car to flee to the UpperWorld, like I first thought.

They did it to show me how to get UnderGround.

That's where the mission starts. UnderGround, in the big city, like my mom said.

I toss the bird into the hole, cup and all, use my tattered Kmart specials to quick kick the dirt back over it.

"What're you doing?" Haze says. "Tosh. You look deranged."

"I gotta go."

"Go?" He steps over the shovel handle, follows me back inside the trailer. "Go where?"

I beeline for my room, grab my messenger bag, stuff it full of socks and underwear, my phone charger, a half-eaten bag of cheesy snack mix. And the gum pack with my mom's note inside.

"Where are you going?"

"UnderGround."

"*What?*"

I dash back down the hall, out the door, hop down the steps toward the street.

"What underground?" Haze calls after me.

"New York," I tell him, because if I say the Boneyard, he'll restrain me to a chair with plastic zip ties until I come to my senses. Besides, it's not a lie to say New York. That's where the entrance to the UnderWorld is. I know that now.

Haze grabs my arm. "Dude, you *are* crazy!" he shouts within an inch of my face. The word swipes at me, stings across my skin. "You've barely even left your house since—"

I shove against him to keep him from finishing the thought, watch through the goggles as he stumbles backward.

He's surprised, I can tell, surprised and maybe a little hurt. But I don't care. He doesn't seem too worried about who *he* hurts by saying stupid shit like that.

Even though he's pissed, Haze follows me as I stumble-run down the street.

As he barrages me with questions I have no intention of answering, I spot what I'm looking for. There, on Clinton just off Buchanan. Not the same yellow car, but a taxicab-yellow *Termi-Pest* truck with its mutantly larger-than-life cockroach on top and the company motto painted along the side.

COCKROACHES ARE OUR SPECIALTY.

Yeah. Only now cockroaches are *my* specialty.

I swallow my disgust at the sight of that four-foot-long fiber-glass bug perched on top of the truck, channel my inner ninja warrior, and approach the driver's-side door all stealth-like.

"Whoa. What are you doing?"

I make a visual sweep of the perimeter before peeking inside the window. Just as I figured: the keys are in the ignition.

I reach for the door handle, but Haze tackle-pins me to the truck.

"Whatever you're thinking about doing?" he says. "Don't."

I try a Roundhouse move to get him off me. But he pushes harder, hard enough to make my shoulders burn against the siding.

"This is a bad idea, Tosh. You're not thinking this through. You don't even know how to drive."

"The hell. We took drivers' ed together."

"We never actually *drove* a car."

"We used the simulators," I hiss through my pain. "Same thing."

"No, it's not." He leans into the shove, and I clench my teeth to keep from grunting in agony. The mantel clock is ticking down on this mission, and I'm starting to panic.

"You're being totally irrational, Tosh."

"You're wrong, *Nate*." Little droplets of spit fly out of my mouth as I utter that one unforgivable word—his real name. We've been last-name-only since fourth grade. "I'm being *totally* rational. I'm doing what you said. *See the world. Live in the now.*"

Haze's face goes blank.

His grip slowly eases from around my arms.

He backs away from me, and even though I know it makes me the biggest dick-friend in the UpperWorld, I turn, unlatch the handle, open the door. Just before I get in, I hear a quick whiz, feel something strike my back and then fall to the road at my feet.

It's his face mask. Haze threw his face mask at me.

Good. I may need it.

I bend down to pick it up.

"If you get in that car and drive away," he says, "you're crazy for sure."

I swing into the seat. "If I stay here, I'm even crazier. I can fix this, Haze."

We stare at each other for a few tense seconds through the open window. I don't want him to try to talk me out of anything. Because he's right—there are potentially hundreds of reasons I shouldn't do this and only one solid reason why I should.

To Ascend.

I throw the truck into drive and screech off toward the UnderWorld.

– 5.5 –

The commandos made it look so easy when they hopped in that fat yellow car and shot off down the abandoned highway. I fix the scene in my mind exactly the way I saw it on the computer, try to copy their moves to the nth degree.

I mean, it's just driving.

How hard can it be?

– 6 –

Cruising down the empty streets of Sandusky is pretty snap.

Taking the turns? Nothing snap about that. I'm gonna need special ops just to keep the truck in the center of the lane.

My eyes drift over to the passenger's seat, catch sight of my cell phone and Haze's painter's mask sitting where his ass would be if he were any kind of friend. At a stop sign, I take the mask, place it over the empty headrest. There. Now it's more like Haze is riding shotgun. For some reason, that calms me down.

Do you have any idea how far it is from Sandusky to New York?

I cast another glance at the mask before peeling away from the stop sign.

"Five hundred and seventeen miles," I say. "It's for a good cause, though."

You just committed grand-theft auto. How could that possibly be for a good cause?

"I'm a first timer with no criminal record. What's one little felony?"

One little felony means spending the best years of your life in jail.

That's the thing about jail. You can already be locked up in a certain way and no one else would ever know.

This better be important, Tosh. You'd better be on a mission to save the world.

"Something like that."

And while we're on it, could you have stolen a more conspicuous car? I mean, you're driving a bright yellow truck with a gigantic bug on top. And you have five hundred and fifteen miles to go. Does that not alarm you?

"Actually, no," I say. It's true, too. There's no way to articulate how *not* alarmed I am at this moment. Haze is with me—my posse, the real one, the guy who knows the hell I've been through for the past 1,586-plus days. Who saw the first signs of cataclysm from the go-kart seat next to mine. This is one raid I need him with me on. Cam is loyal to the game, sure; he knows the Boneyard like his own backyard, and that's worth something. But Haze knows *me*, and that's worth everything.

I reach for the knob on the radio.

Keep your eyes on the road.

"It's too quiet. I need something in my head."

Well, that's accurate.

It's not accurate, though. My head isn't empty; it's full of chaos right now. I usually pour some Motor City or Bunny Puke into my ear to solve that problem.

I take one hand off the wheel, unwrap my headphones, pop a single earbud in, and hit play.

What are you doing?

"Clearing the fog."

I'm pretty sure that everything you're doing right now is against the law.

I don't tell Haze, but wearing an illegal earbud is the least of my worries. If I were him, I'd be more concerned that I'm chasing a cockroach on a quest to turn back the clock. Me, Caleb Tosh, trying to become Worthy so I can keep the UpperWorld from self-destructing.

If that doesn't have "superfail" written all over it, I don't know what does.

By my math-lame calculations, it'll take about nine hours to drive five hundred and seventeen miles to New York City, and since I've never done anything for nine hours except game, I'm pretty sure that the next leg of my life is going to drag solid ass. Bunny Puke helps drown out most of the unwanted noise: the sounds of a raid I couldn't finish, the screams of grim panic, the click-and-report of my worst fail ever, the eruption and fallout of a total wipe.

I squeeze my eyes together, lift the goggles to clear the beads of fog off the lenses.

That's when my phone starts going nuts on the seat next to me. I tick my eyes at Haze's face mask, knowing what he'd say if he were really here, then grab the phone anyway and open my messages by rote memory. My eyes dart between the screen and the road so I can see who it is, as if I don't already know. It's either the cockroach or the commandos, and if it's them, I'd like to read their instructions without pile-driving into a guardrail.

Avoid the toll.

That's it? That's the big instruction, *avoid the toll?* How do they expect me to do that? There's pretty much one way to get to New York from Ohio, and it's a straight shot. I look back at the screen to make sure I read it right.

Yep.

You're texting behind the wheel?

"Well, *you* weren't gonna answer it." I thumb through the app icons on the screen.

What are you doing, Tosh?

Devin. The go-karts. On a mission to save—

"I need to figure out how to avoid the tolls."

Man, I can't believe you're texting. You don't even have a license!

"You're not exactly being helpful right now, Haze. Besides, I need to get off this highway, fast. Can you at least tell me when I get to the app with the car on it?"

I don't know how to use that thing.

"You don't have to. Just tell me when I hit the right icon." My thumb dances across the screen.

You don't have the best track record behind the wheel, Tosh. Watch the road.

"I am, but just tell me when I get to the car."

There.

I sneak a peek.

"Not the map," I say, leaning over. "The car!"

Damn it, Tosh. Keep your eyes on the road!

"I need to get off this highway, *now!*" I take the phone back into my own airspace, watch the icons as I zip through them to get to the car app. I don't know where it is since I don't drive and therefore have never needed to use it.

Tosh, the road . . .

"I'm almost there."

Tosh! The road!

The world outside the truck hovers for a few seconds, then kicks into stop-motion. Trees and asphalt and truck and sky flash-flicker past. I have no idea how long it takes for the Termi-Pest truck to finish rolling and come to an upright stop on the side of the highway, but eventually it does.

I may have blacked out for a second or two.

When I manage to get my eyes open, my head fills with dense fog. It's the truck, I realize; the truck is belching smoke from under the accordion-fold of the hood. For a split second I think I may have forgotten to use my seat belt, which would be bad . . . very bad. I could be ejected, injured, lying on the highway having a surreal, out-of-body experience.

A frantic dig reveals the belt strap tangled up in my T-shirt.

And then I look over, see Haze twisted into an impossible shape against the door. I barely remember him coming with me, but he must have, right? Yeah. Riding shotgun, giving me all kinds of crap about using my phone while driving . . .

I rush to unbuckle before spinning around in a panic to see if he's okay.

His head is tipped back at a weird angle against the window.

"*Oh God . . .*" I rip the gas mask off his face, slap his cheek as hard as I can. I don't know what that's supposed to accomplish, but they do it on TV all the time.

Haze doesn't react.

Instead of being concerned that he might have a broken neck or some other potentially paralyzing injury, I do what any clear-thinking person would do in a moment of crisis. I slap him again.

Because I should have . . . with Devin . . . I just couldn't move.

This can't happen again. I *need* Haze. I can't let him—

"What the hell?" he sputters.

He's all green. I got him back just in time.

"You passed out during the accident," I say.

"What accident?"

The question echoes dull and flat in the too-still air.

We both sit up, look around in a daze.

I wonder why we don't hear sirens yet.

As the smoke starts to clear, I peek in the rearview mirror, expecting a squadron of cop cars and ambulances to roll up behind us any second. But all I see is the cockroach, dislodged, lying on its back, several yards behind us. Good. The best kind of UnderWorld mob is a dead one.

Plenty more where that came from, though. I can't allow the confusion of the moment to distract me from the very real need to brace myself for the coming battle.

"What are we supposed to do now?" Haze asks.

The question pushes the little hairs at the back of my neck into their full upright position. I don't know what happens now. I look down at my phone, hoping the commandos will dial in any second with further instructions.

Haze's breath wheezes through those filtered chambers so hard I feel my own lungs starting to burn.

"Tosh?"

"Grab your things," I say.

"What things?"

"There's an overpass up ahead."

The highways in the Boneyard are full of overpasses, but you have to be careful; they're prime hideaways for minion soldiers. They can also lead UnderGround, but that's dicey too. A lot of those tunnels are traps.

I pull my messenger bag out from behind the seat and open the driver's side door, which immediately sags off its now-broken hinges. Haze just sits there, staring at me openmouthed while I head down the shoulder of the highway.

He breaks the brittle silence by launching into a rant about how dangerous this joyride is and how reckless I am, his words chasing me down from all the way back at the truck. He keeps on ranting as he slides off the seat, as he slams the door behind him, as he marches down the shoulder and around the curve in the road. Phrases like "completely lost your mind" and "undeniably insane" collide in midair with the jagged puffs of smoke drifting in our direction.

Haze manages to catch up with me, but that's because for the last minute or so I've been on lockdown, my feet bolted in shock to a single spot on the cracked pavement.

He wanders into the middle of the freeway to meet me, where we stand in complete silence and just . . . stare.

"How'd we miss *this*?" he finally whispers, leaning in to me like he's afraid someone might overhear. Which we can now clearly see is impossible.

"It just . . . popped up," I say. "Totally out of nowhere."

Wisps of smoke drag my words away from me, and I follow their tracks to the wreckage up ahead.

"How many cars?" I ask.

"Fifty," he says. "A hundred. Hard to tell."

"Where do you think everyone went?"

"No idea." Haze adjusts his gas mask, and for the first time ever, I covet that thing, wish I had one of my own. The reek of burnt rubber and axle grease and barbecued engine parts hangs heavy in the air.

But the fear . . . the fear of what this could all mean pulls at me like triple gravity.

I try to ignore the brewing sickness in my stomach as we pick our way through the tangle of twisted bumpers, stray hubcaps, curls of tire tread, and corrugated chassis. I half expect, half dread the sound of dying moans from people trapped underneath it all. But the only sound we hear is hissing radiator steam. Beyond that, it's eerie silence.

That is, until the frantic screech of tires heads our way. Haze and I stop dead in our tracks, turn in unison toward the sound. It doesn't help that we're walking right down the middle of the highway; and as the shriek of faulty brakes gets closer, we press ourselves up against an abandoned frozen-foods delivery truck that's tipped at a dicey angle.

The car stops within a few feet of us, and Haze and I brace ourselves for the hail of machine-gun fire that's bound to come spraying out of its blacked-out windows. I wince in anticipation.

But instead the window rolls down, and when it does, my fear starts to melt, then slide, down the side of the frozen-foods delivery truck. Haze pulls his mask under his chin, his mouth hinged open.

"What the hell is happening?" he whispers to me.

I would have asked him the same thing if he hadn't beaten me to it.

- 6.5 -

The driver is a ginger supreme. She has this huge smile, and hair the color of a rusted fender bouncing around her like a shampoo commercial, and long, slender fingers wrapped around the gearshift of the most ghetto car I've ever seen with a savory girl behind the wheel. I mean, the car's a real Frankenstein. But the girl . . . the girl is undeniably hot. And she's here.

Here.

The only other soul in this miles-wide radius of wreckage.

Why is that?

− 7 −

"**It took me about** five passes," she says, panting yet smiling in satisfaction. "But I finally figured out how to get onto the highway without ending up in the bone pile."

Haze and I bank a quick glance off each other, then switch back over to the girl.

"It's the on-ramp," she says. "You have to take the right on-ramp or you're gonna end up crashing into all that." She lifts her arm and points to the massive pileup, as if there might be some confusion as to what she means by "all that."

"We weren't entering the highway when we crashed," I tell her. "We were already on it."

Her face washes over pink, then red. "Oh, was that your truck back there?"

"Yeah. It just started rolling all of a sudden."

Haze fake coughs. "There was nothing all-of-a-sudden about it, Tosh. You took your eyes off the road." I jump in, try to explain about the car icon and avoiding the tolls, but he's hell-bent on splitting hairs here. "You took your hands off the wheel and your eyes off the road."

"That's a no-no," she says.

I narrow my gaze at her. "Who are you?" I ask.

"Oh, I'm sorry." She extends her long, slender hand through the open window. "I'm Elan. Of course, that's not my given name. It's my taken name."

"He's got a taken name too." I jab my thumb at Haze, who knocks it out of the way.

"And who are the two of you?"

"Caleb Tosh. Nathan Hayes."

"Just Haze," he says, and I can tell by his voice that he's irritable.

There couldn't be a more inappropriate time to verify how hot this girl is. Like UnderWorld-hostage babe kind of hot.

Wait a second . . .

Did they send her? Did the commandos send this girl to me? Could she be a hostage? I can't tell if I'm supposed to save her, or if she's part of my platoon.

Do not question the mission.

"Well?" she says. "Are you getting in or aren't you?"

I answer with a nod and the gut feeling that everything is suddenly, inexplicably right in the world.

"Yeah. We're all in, sure."

Haze edges me aside. "Don't you think we should find out something about her before we get in her car? Something minuscule, like where she's going?"

"I told you," I whisper back. "We're going to New York."

"*She* could be going anywhere," he says, but I push him around to the passenger's side of the car and through the open door.

I let him sit up front with Elan so I can stare at her without being too obvious about it. She looks familiar, but I can't place her. I may have rescued her before, but in her civvies, it would be hard to tell.

Elan gives Haze the once-over. I can see it through the rear-view mirror.

"So what's with the gas mask, potato chip?" she finally asks.

"Just in case."

She nods as if this makes perfect sense to her.

"And where do you all hail from?"

Haze and I answer in unison, only I blurt out "Sandusky" and he mumbles "Cincinnati," and as I shove the butt of my hand against the back of his ski-knit head, Elan goes, "You boys are gonna have to get your story straight."

"No kidding," I mumble.

She adjusts the mirror, locks sights on me.

"Big city?" she asks.

Our eyes connect in the mirror, and I start to sweat from a surge of heat blasting in from nowhere.

Her smile is 100 percent evaporated.

There's no way she could know about that note in the gum pack buried in my messenger bag. The list. My mom's list. She'd scrawled those exact words: "big city."

I blink the sting of sweat out of my eyes.

"Where are *you* going?" I ask.

She flips her hair over her shoulders. "Or should I say, Big Apple?"

Haze's head pivots in slow motion over his shoulder. Even through his shades, I can tell he's staring at me, and all I can do is avoid staring back. If he wants to know how she knew that, I don't have a way to answer him.

I take out my phone, nervously switch playlists, check and recheck my home screen. There's got to be another message coming, more info, any little scrap of assistance from the commandos, since it's their fault we got thrown off course here in the first place, thanks to their little "avoid the toll" debacle.

Unless this is all part of the mission I'm not supposed to question.

Still, I can't shake the preraid sensation of static electricity snap-crackling through my body. Can't get my foot to stop nervous-bouncing against the floorboard of Elan's car, which is decomposing to the point that I worry I might bounce a hole straight through the bottom of it.

I start fake keying the words "save it" over and over again on my phone, but when I look down at the screen, the low-battery icon is flashing in the corner. I shut down all the apps, pop out the earbud, and lean forward in the seat.

"Can I charge up?"

"Anything you want, potato chip."

Haze reaches back, takes the phone and charger from me,

plugs it all in. I almost can't believe the cigarette lighter still works in this crap car.

Only now my hands are twitchy. No keypad, no music, no Snipe page, no way to check messages. And five hundred miles to go.

I close my eyes. Why the hell wasn't the old man at Goofy Golf with Devin? How could he just disappear like that, not even leave a note? Wouldn't he know? Wouldn't he know that would trip my shit in the worst possible way? After my mom and Stan . . . You don't just up and leave without—

I replay the conversation with the commandos over and over in my mind. What did I miss? Were there secret plans, messages, hints I should have taken note of? *We think you can be of help to us.* If that's the case, where *are* they?

My head jerks against the tattered seat back. I sit up, look around, scratch a rogue itch.

"Hey," I say to no one in particular. "Hand me my phone."

Elan is the one who pops it out, charger and all, and I immediately check the wall screen, where the Day-Glo numbers pulse neon green at me.

Sweat starts sheeting down my back.

Midnight.

It's already midnight.

That can't be. When I handed my phone to Haze, it said ten to four. No way that was eight hours ago.

I bolt upright in the seat, pivot toward the window, then each of the other windows, but no matter where I look, it's all the same darkness.

"Haze!" I call out.

His head wobbles off the back of the seat. "Wha—?"

I recant. Everything's *not* right with the world. In fact, it would be accurate to say that something here is very, very wrong.

"Where are we?" I ask.

Elan's smile reflects back at me through the rearview mirror, her teeth glowing in the light of a massive full moon.

"You mean, are we there yet?"

"Are we *where* yet?" I'm testing her. I know it. She knows it. Haze . . . whatever. Waking up is not his forte.

Elan hasn't answered my question, so I press against the window, squint to get a look at the full-frontal urban assault: honking horns, sirens, traffic. The night spasms to life around us, puking up neon and humanity everywhere I look.

"Are we *here* yet," she corrects me. "And the answer is, yes."

I don't know how Haze and I both sawed enough z's to get from Ohio to New York, assuming we are, in fact, *in* New York, without even noticing the extensive passage of time. That alone is enough to roll me, especially since Haze is a natural-born conspiracy theorist and I already know he doesn't trust this girl.

My own mistrust increases exponentially as the city presses its grimy face against the windows of the car.

"This is where I drop you boys off," she says, winding her way through a tangle of crowded streets.

I kick another glance out the window, absorb the sheer volume of bodies and machinery and high-rises and steam and neon and rebar and asphalt.

The commandos had better chime in here soon.

"Off you go," she says. "The universe abhors a vacuum, you know. Once you leave home, you have to turn up somewhere."

Haze and I stagger out of her decrepit little car, and as we step onto the curb, I remember about the UnderGround, the City Hall Station.

I turn, call out, "Wait, where's the—"

But the Big Apple has already taken a bite out of the night, and just like that, both the girl and the car are gone.

- 7.5 -

I'm not sure why the commandos would send an UnderWorld hostage to me and then have her drive off without being saved.

So, fine, this isn't a salvation mission. But why have Elan show up just in the nick of time and take us exactly where we needed to go, and then, just before I could think of how to help her, *poof?*

Gone.

− 8 −

Haze's mirror-eyed rage bears down on me with an intensity I am not expecting.

"It's really no sweat," I say, wiping beads of perspiration off my upper lip. "We just need to find the—"

"It took us *fifteen minutes* to get from Ohio to New York," he cuts in. "How is that no sweat?"

"No, it didn't." I flip up the bottoms of the yellow goggles to let them defog. "It only seems like it because we were sleeping."

"Exactly. Sleeping. Both of us. *For nine hours.*"

"You have *narcolepsy*, Haze." It's true. He does. Haze has some kind of stress-induced narcolepsy. Why *I* stayed asleep for the better part of five hundred miles is still pretty sketch.

"I don't think narcolepsy explains a nine-hour nap," he says.

"You don't think what we've been through today qualifies as an ordeal?"

Something knocks against my shoe as we walk, derailing my train of thought.

I sidestep it to see what it is, and the city floods my head, bending light and sound into unrecognizable shards and fractals.

I reach down good and slow, clamp it between the tips of two fingers.

It's the drink cup. Not *a* drink cup. *The* drink cup. From the go-kart track. The one I buried the bird in behind our trailer in Sandusky, Ohio. And yeah, I know there must be a trillion green and yellow drink cups in the Big Apple.

But how many of them still have a blackbird feather inside?

I stare into the mangled cup, gawk at its contents.

"That's foul," Haze says.

My heart beats out tribal drum chants as I pull it out, flip it between my fingers a couple of times.

learn to fly

fly away

As Haze scouts out our surroundings, I quick stash the feather before he notices. It's definitely the strangest item on my Trade Screen, but there must be some reason to have it, or else why would it have been put there?

I turn the drink cup over, looking for the words I already know I'll see.

Subway. City Hall Station.

Motor City pumps tinny and low into my left ear. The sharp riff of the guitar solo on their heavy-metal anthem pierces through my brain waves as a siren wails in the near distance, and it occurs to me: this isn't an address. It's an instruction.

I pull up SnipeSearch on my phone.

"What are you looking for?" Haze asks.

I show him the address on the cup, and he flinches in disgust.

"Throw that thing away, man."

We stumble along, following the landmarks and reading the warnings that come up on the page about how the station is closed to the general public, how you have to make an appointment to tour the tunnels, and how it would be a massive breach of security to go down there unaccompanied by the proper authorities, since the station is situated right under City Hall.

And then, just off to one side, I spot the entrance.

Of course, it's surrounded by a soaring chain-link fence and a gate that's dead-bolted with several Magnum-grade padlocks.

Haze goes slack in front of the gate. "Well, this steams."

"There's gotta be a way in," I say, mostly to myself.

"I just want to clarify that we're not meant to go down there. You know that, right?"

I don't blame him. He doesn't understand how important any of this is, that going underground is mission critical. He doesn't know how any of this works; he's never technically been to the Boneyard before.

But I have. And I know there's got to be a way in, an on-ramp, as Elan called it.

"Even if we do get in, we won't be able to see anything down there, Tosh. Not even the rats running across our feet, and that's saying something because New York rats weigh ten pounds apiece."

Point taken.

I dig into my bag for a penlight I can't find, my fingers brushing against the feather instead. A fat knot of exhaust fumes and urban funk sticks in my throat, refusing to be swallowed away. I have to get down there. No plan B, no alternative route. It's UnderGround or mission failure. Period.

A text message buzzes at me, and I'm so sure it's the commandos with instructions for how to break in that I open the app without thinking.

The world below will weep blood, it says. There's an attachment, of course. It's the cockroach.

A low groan cuts loose from my gut. Turk seems to know my every move. I'm starting to wonder how it'll ever matter if I crack the tunnel code; that bastard will always be able to stay ahead of me.

Clearly, I'm not getting an assist here. I'm sure the commandos brought me this far courtesy of Elan, but telling me about *the world below* isn't much help. I'll have to figure out how to go UnderGround myself.

I pace the length of the fence.

"Dead bolts," Haze says. "Doesn't that just figure."

Roundhouse would have something in his bag he could use for bolt cutters. What do I have? Socks and underwear and a gum pack with a note inside.

I stop midpace, scan the length of the fence again, quicker this time.

sneak in

That's what her note said.

I pull at the fence. It's secured every few feet with wire ties, but I tug the length of it in the direction of the gate, and there, just at the end, it gives.

The corner isn't secured.

Haze and I stare at each other in disbelief. *Easy,* I'm thinking. *Way too easy.* I'm this close to chickening out when the next message comes through.

The end is near.

And then one more:

Save it.

- 9 -

We slip through the opening in the fence, into the station entrance and down the stairs to the abandoned terminal.

"We shouldn't have been able to do that," Haze says, his voice bouncing back to us in echoes. I pull the penlights I was looking for out of my bag, knowing they'll be no match against the expansive black of the UnderGround.

"Never mind," I say. "Just hold the beam low and steady and keep moving."

It's wet in the tunnel, smells like ocean or moss one minute, urine and garbage the next, and so dark that the only thing we can rely on the penlights for is to make sure we're not stepping on the ten-pound rats Haze talked about. I reach out my hand, run it along the brick wall as a guide. But pretty soon all I can focus on is the condensation and grime on the tiles, and the next thing I know, my finger hits something flat and hard and ovoid.

Something that does not feel like tile.

Before I can pull away, the protrusion scampers over the tips of my fingers, and I emit some sort of other-than-human sound that echoes perfectly through the catacomb. Haze spins around, shining his penlight on the wall, where he tracks the biggest fucking cockroach I've ever seen in my life.

"Sweet Jesus," Haze says. "Did you see that? It was a tank!"

"Yes, I saw it. Shut up and keep moving."

Haze busts a gut, not realizing what this cockroach sighting could actually mean.

"Poor thing is probably running back to its little roach friends right now, going, *Oh my God, I can't get the human stank off me!*" He makes some squeaky little noises, which I think are meant to emulate a cockroach.

"It's not funny," I say.

The phone kicks a text message into my pocket, but I'm too rattled by what just happened to pick up another picture of Turk. He would totally do that—send a minion scout into the catacomb and then chase it with a picture of himself to remind me who's really in charge here.

"How is that not funny?" Haze is saying, a chuckle still twinging his voice. "Why is it that nothing with an exoskeleton seems to garner much of a—"

But before Haze can finish the thought, we stop in unison, let our gazes slide up the station walls. We've reached an atrium of sorts, an arachnidian juncture of subway tunnels that all seem to converge right here. The domed roof is actually a series of skylights, with neon and moonbeams pouring down on us through the panes. There's enough ambient light coming in through the once-blackened windows that we can see traces of long-ago grandeur in the tunnels—gilded brickwork, glass tiles, brass chandeliers.

"Holy mother of . . ."

The UnderWorld looks nothing like this on the crappy screen of the Relic. Maybe this isn't even the UnderWorld. There are no burning wall sconces, no armed guards patrolling. *The world below will weep with blood.* I look up. Nope. Not even that.

I pocket my earbuds so I can listen for sounds of an impending incursion—soldiers, minion raiders, anything to indicate that we're at least on the right track.

I squint to see down one of the tunnel arms, but it's too dark to see anything beyond the dome. I've never experienced the tunnels from this vantage point—I'm all turned around, no longer sure of the code sequence. All I know is, if I take the tunnels in the wrong order, *we'll* be the ones running back out onto the highway in flames.

I stop. Turn.

It's the on-ramp, Elan had said. *You have to take the right on-ramp or you're gonna end up crashing into—*

"I knew it," I say, tasting the rank air is it rushes into my open mouth. "One of these tunnels is definitely the way in. We have to figure out the sequence from inside. Bastard has me all twisted around."

Haze is so busy gawking at all the history, he probably doesn't even hear me.

I let my gaze drag down the sides of the walls to the other

arms that feed into the atrium. As my vision adjusts, it reveals even more skylights stretching down the tubes at regular intervals. This is Russian roulette. I already wiped this level once before, so spectacularly I almost got kicked out of the Boneyard for good because of it. I need mappers. And some dps wouldn't hurt either. Something tells me I'm gonna want to wreck some shit pretty soon.

I close my eyes, strain my ears to superhuman, hoping for any small clue, signal, direction.

I walk toward one of the tunnel openings, face the undiluted darkness. The old arms of the tracks seem closed off and stuffier than under the dome, by a hefty factor. Sweat dribbles down the sides of my face, trickles into my ears, fogs up my goggles; I can't even imagine what it's like for Haze in that knit cap and painter's mask. If ever there was a time he'd want to let that shit go, you'd think it'd be now.

I squint into the void. Is this the one? Getting it wrong could be lethal.

I made that mistake before. Split decision. Wrong choice. Devin. Max damage. I need to fix it. I need to know if this is the beginning of the end.

Or the end of it.

The answer comes as a low rumble at first. But as the noise and movement gain momentum, the dimness of the tunnel shrinks in proportion, and suddenly I realize that all that separates me and Haze from an oncoming subway car is a few measly inches of wall space.

"*Run!*" I scream. Which is a ridiculous thing to say, if you think about it. No one should ever have to tell you to run if a train is barreling down on you.

Haze and I sprint our asses off as the sound and the heat and the shaking get louder, hotter, nearer. I have never run this hard or this fast in my life; in fact, I've never had to run for my life. Now would be the worst possible moment for a text to buzz through.

I refuse to answer it. It's either Turk, trying to distract me so I get flattened, or the commandos—and if it's them, well, screw their lousy timing and their better-late-than-never—

Hold up.

I got a message earlier that I never looked at. What if that one was something like, *Watch out for the subway car!* and there it is, sitting unread in my back pocket as I get smashed on the abandoned tracks under City Hall?

A sprint or two later, we're back in the atrium and safely on the platform, where I yank the phone out of my back pocket and slide it open.

The world beneath will weep blood.

I look up. The atrium has gotten hot. Melt-my-bones hot.

Sweet Jesus. I'm sweating, Haze is sweating; even the walls are sweating.

The walls. Are sweating.

Not water.

Not condensation.

Blood.

- 10 -

The deep blast of a honking subway train nearly shoots me out of my own skin. I haven't even had time to process the dark red ooze dripping down the walls of the catacombs, but Haze and I spin around, and there, not ten feet away, is a shrunken-down version of a subway car.

And it's waiting. For us.

"What the hell is this?" Haze says. "It said on your app they haven't run trains on these tracks in over a hundred—"

"Just get in." I push him through the open door of the car and scramble in behind him.

So it wasn't the tunnels—it was never *meant* to be the tunnels. It was the actual subway: *this* is our on-ramp. The mission hasn't even started yet.

Within seconds, we're moving, our pint-sized train car negotiating through the tight-cornered tracks like an amusement-park ride. Ages-old brass chandeliers flicker as we pass by, eerily illuminating the tunnel walls until they're just how I remember the Boneyard to look.

"Yo, Tosh."

I follow the trajectory of Haze's shaky finger.

The thick humidity that's strong-armed its way into the subway car by now is still dripping in bloodred rivulets down the tiled walls of the station tunnels.

"That's dire, man," he says, and I feel a stab of guilt. He can't even begin to conceptualize what we're sitting in the middle of.

The air around us is dense, heavy with the smell of wet cement and garbage. A metallic tang leeches off the walls of the subway car, burns my lungs every time I inhale.

My vision goes into soft focus, drifts mothlike through the car. I shouldn't be too pissed at the commandos for not keeping in better communication. Chat windows won't be secure. Texting is the only method they can use, and it's not very convenient. Still, I have to remember, they're getting me where I need to go. I just have to remain vigilant. Turk and his army are clearly lying in wait. Watching. Listening.

Outside the window, the shimmering skyline blinks in and out of view. A cast-off glow of neon-yellow streetlights illuminates my reflection in the glass and then too easily disappears. I feel the void in the center of my chest, the ache of being there one second and gone the next. If I don't fix things, everything I know could blink out of view that way. For good this time.

The train takes a sharp dip, dragging my stomach down with it, and suddenly we're underground again. With sweat-slick fingers, I pop in an earbud so I don't have to hear the screech of the subway tracks. Still, I keep a close eye out the window, hoping for some hint of where we're headed, since no one seems too keen on telling me.

"Tosh?" I hear Haze whisper.

He's pressed so flat against the window it's almost funny—until I turn to see what he's on about.

The bricks of the tunnel zip by us faster and faster, like a scene out of one of those sci-fi movies where the spaceship hits warp speed and the stars turn into blurred lines that shoot out behind it.

"What the—" But before he can finish the thought, he drops off the grid again. Narcoleptic Haze, succumbing to blissful slumber.

I close my eyes too, wishing I could lean my head back against the window and grab a quick nap. Not a good idea, unless I'm willing to sustain a third-degree concussion as the subway car caroms through the winding tunnels.

Sometimes she'd take me with her on her drive-offs. We wouldn't talk. I'd just lay my head against the window and let the vibration of the car soothe me. She liked having the company, I could tell, even though she never said it. I guess by then she was too used to keeping all her thoughts to herself.

I dig into my pocket, fish out the blackbird feather, flip it between my fingers. I left today without knowing where Devin was. I'm not saying it doesn't matter; it matters. But when I finally reach Turk's lair, when I kill that hostage-taking sonofabitch, it'll undo all the mistakes I made, and Devin won't need me to protect him like that anymore. He'll go back to being the emo skate-boarding, arm-punching, cheesy-snack-stealing punk he always was, and everything will be exactly the way it should be.

When I close my eyes again, I see the blood schussing through my veins like this subway car, fueled by anger and no small dose of fear.

They told me to save it. They're giving me another chance. I have to get it right this time, even if it kills me.

I pull out my phone just to give my nervous hands something to do, realize I can't check anything—my apps are going haywire, random-flashing the icons on my wall screen. Doesn't that just figure. Nothing's fixed right now; nothing is static. Even time is meaningless now that I'm in the Boneyard; never mind that I can still hear it *tick-tick-ticking* right through my headphones.

The end is near.

The words flash bright neon green above my head.

An unexpected vibration cuts straight through the jarring chaos of the subway. Shocked, I quick pull up the message.

Time means nothing.

"Well, that's helpful," I say.

Time unused melts into pools of regret.

Swell.

"What ever happened to *The world beneath will weep blood?*" I say out loud. Weep blood, my ass. I guess if you want to get techni-cal, the walls of the station were kind of "bleeding," but that was just a screen trick, if you ask me. Any moron could see it was condensation making some centuries-old funk run down the tiles. Not blood at all—just vaguely blood*like*.

Haze has been sound asleep all this time, but the piercing wail of metal on metal rips through the car as we careen to a stop, and he sputters back into consciousness.

He pulls the face mask down under his chin.

"Where are we?"

"Cinderella's castle," I say, throwing my bag over my shoulder.

The car spasms to a stop and the door wheezes open. I follow Haze outside just as the first dim light of morning bleaches the horizon.

The truth is, I don't know where we are. But I do know without even looking that the subway car is already gone.

I fully expect Haze to fire an Uzi round of questions at me, but he doesn't. We just start walking down the narrow, deserted street, lined with half-dead trees and decrepit, abandoned buildings whose busted-out windows lie shattered under our feet. The crunch of debris against concrete is the only sound we hear as we kick our way through piles of twisted window frames, chunks of Sheetrock and plywood, two-by-fours sprouting rusted nails, a decaying bird carcass lying in the gutter.

Time unused melts into pools of regret.

"I'd kill for a Mountain Dew," I blurt out.

"Coffee. Same here."

Even so, we pass several convenience stores and diners without ever stopping to go in. Most of the places don't even look open.

I'm starting to second-guess the decision to come down here

without the smallest brigade. I'm not talking about Haze. Haze is my man. He's my shit-caller. I mean, the guy calls me out on my shit at every single turn. But he can't crush a tank on my behalf, or take out a roach mob or cause max damage when the time comes. Haze doesn't know the rules of engagement here.

The road widens and the negative space around us begins to fill in—run-down cars, more empty buildings, brown-gray daylight.

Around a corner, Haze and I stop short in unison, let our gaze slide up the length of the concrete facade of an unfamiliar building. A dozen or so stories of rust-colored brick rise to meet the sharp-angled patina roof as rows and rows of paneless windows gape back at us like a blank stare.

Vacant eyes. Boarded-up mouth. No way in. Devin. A wave of sickness shoots through me.

Should have at least brought a Medic.

"I bet you're going to tell me you want to go in," Haze says.

"Yep."

I have no idea what this place is, only that if I don't go inside, I'll have left something undone.

"Notice how the doors and windows on the bottom floor are all bricked up?" he says.

"Yeah, but look right above it." I point to the two arched windows that flank the entrance of the building. The windows are bricked in, true, but the holes above them aren't.

"Someone's gotten in here who wasn't supposed to," I tell Haze. "The question is, how?"

"*That's* the question, Tosh? Not, why do you want to commit breaking and entering, or what we're even doing here in the first place?"

sneak in

I'm here to sneak in. That's what her note said.

But I can't make the words come out.

Haze shakes his head. "Elan was right, man. One of us needs to get his story straight."

Elan . . .

I tip my head back, fix my gaze on the busted window openings for a long, wondering moment.

"Hey!" I yell at last. "Hey, up there!"

Haze turns eleven shades of white. "Man, what are you doing? This is an abandoned—"

Three scraggly heads of black hair pop out of the windows before he gets to the end of the sentence. None of them is Elan, though, so there goes that theory.

"What's with the yelling?" one of the guys shouts down to us.

"We need a place to squat," I call back. No idea where that came from.

The heads disappear, and for a moment Haze and I just stand there like a couple of jackasses, cutting our stupefied gazes between the building and each other. But then the one guy tosses something out the window, and it only takes me a second to realize it's a rope ladder.

He wants us to climb up.

"That doesn't look very sturdy," Haze says, and even though I'm thinking the same thing, I don't let on.

I hoist my messenger bag over my shoulder and grab on to both sides of the ladder. The swaying does nothing to reassure me; if anything, it makes the rope feel even flimsier in my hands than it looked flopping out the window.

"Dude—"

"Haze, shut up," I say. "If you make one rational argument about why I shouldn't climb up, I'll totally chicken out, and I *can't* chicken out now—got it?"

I wait out the split second of festering silence before he says the one thing I need to hear him say more than anything else in the universe.

"Sure, Tosh. Whatever you need to do."

I start to climb, forced to acknowledge something I should have considered before sticking my foot through the first rung. I have z-e-r-o upper-body strength. Sad fact: there's nothing remotely like a defined muscle group anywhere on Caleb Tosh's body.

"You'd better hurry," the dude in the window says. "They can't bust you once you're in here, but they can bust you while you're climbing."

"Go!" Haze says.

I roll my eyes as the hellish memories of gym class parade before them. No amount of creative visualization can block out the thought that Haze has a backside view of my frayed, one-size-too-big jeans as I climb. Not to mention the dude in the window gets to watch me nearly stroke out while I struggle for the opening.

The dude inside sticks his arm out. "Here, grab me," he says.

I clasp him around the wrist and he does the same, and before I know it, he's managed to pull me all the way inside. I lay panting on the ground, cushioned in a thick layer of dust and reeling from the shock of physical exertion.

I can hear the guy working to get Haze up the ladder, a feat that probably requires a lot less effort for him than it did for me. But I'm not even watching. My eyes are squeezed shut as I fight to catch my breath.

From the sound of things, Haze has just toppled unceremoniously into the room.

"Tosh." His voice spins through the filters of his mask. "You okay?"

"Yeah." I sit up, open my eyes, look around.

Sure enough, there's Haze leaning up against the wall under the window, with his hands plastered against his knit cap like he's trying to keep his head from popping off.

I turn and survey the now up-close faces of the threesome: two guys and a girl, all covered in a thin layer of dust that matches the thicker layer of dust covering every other square inch of this low-ceilinged space.

"Thanks," I say.

"No problem," the guy from the window says. "We're the Prophets."

My eyebrows ricochet into my hairline as I search my memory for any brigade with that name. Nothing.

"You're who?" I ask.

"The Prophets. Industrial-techno-folk-punk. Lemme guess…" He turns to Haze, sizing up his post-apocalyptic headgear. "Electronic-thrash-reggae?"

A brigade with a backstory. Not sure how I feel about that.

"Naw," I say. "We're just looking for a place to hang out."

"Oh." He slides his gaze back and forth between us a few more times. "I get it. Yeah, that's cool. Lots of rooms here. Very private."

I shoot a confused look at Haze as my brain absorbs the words "very private."

"Not, like, *private*," I say. "We just need to lay low for a while."

"Oh yeah? What are you guys on the run from?" he asks.

Another intriguing question. I stall, trying to think up an answer, and for a few seconds I wonder if we somehow ended up somewhere we didn't intend to go. I don't have a mapper, so it's possible, I guess. But no . . . that's not right. I know this map. I've been here before, tons of times.

I decide to test them.

"We stole a car," I say. "So now we're on the run."

"*You* stole a car," Haze cuts in.

"Right. *I* stole a car, so . . . anyway. We're on the lam now."

"On the lam," the guy says. "Cool."

The girl moves forward, and that's when I notice they all have the same short-cropped, chopped-up, black-dyed hair. They look like mangled crows, to be honest. That'd be a great band name—way better than the Prophets.

The girl's kind of hot.

"I'm Ravyn," she says as I try really hard to hold eye contact with her and not let my eyes drift to her purple bra, which I can clearly see because it shows straight through the thin white fabric of the tank top she's wearing.

Ravyn is curvalicious.

"Tosh," I say. "That's Haze."

Haze, still plastered against the wall, lifts one hand in greeting while holding on to his head with the other.

The window dude comes forward with his arm stretched out. "Eek," he says, giving me one of those multiplex handshakes. "It used to be Zeke, but I ditched the Z, man."

"Sweet," I say.

The other guy throws a peace sign from across the space. He's eating a candy bar, but what I'm really tripping on is that his head almost touches the ceiling. I don't think it's because he's especially tall, though. I just think this is a ridiculously short room.

"I'm Bill," he says.

I nod, wondering what we're supposed to do now that the formalities are over.

"We usually crash in another part of the Castle. You guys coming?" Eek asks.

The Castle?

"Sure." I swivel toward the windows. "Yo, Haze. You coming?"

Haze finally looks up. "Why am I sitting next to a pile of bricks?"

Eek points to an uneven circular hole in the wall between the two perfectly geometric ones. "Crashers," he says. "Bastards have totally laid waste to the Castle. It's a shame, really."

"Aren't you crashers?" Haze asks. There's an edge to his voice that makes me nervous.

"Hell no," Eek says. "We're squatters. And actually, we don't stay here. It's just a really cheap rehearsal space."

"Any idea how much a practice studio costs in this goddamn place?" Bill asks, trying to fish a chunk of candy bar out from between his crooked teeth with a dirty fingernail. I narrow my eyes and study him. He's too nervous. His eyes bulge out too far, his too-long, bony fingers twitch like antennae as they flail around in his mouth.

I'm not sure what kind of mission these guys are on. Nothing like what we're doing—that seems obvious. But I know one thing for absolute: he's their platoon leader. He shouldn't be since he's a jackass, but he is, and there's something about the guy I just don't trust.

"*Any* idea?" he asks again.

"Not a clue," I say.

"An ass-load." Bill holds up the offending nut, flicks it into the air.

I wince in disgust.

"Only problem is," Eek adds, "we're not the only ones. Lots of bands use this building. It's perfect because of all the rooms and the great acoustics. But we have to leave by seven, because school starts at eight."

My eyes go rogue as I try to discreetly make sense of this

last bit of info. They call themselves "bands," not "platoons." Plus they don't give off any kind of studious vibe whatsoever.

"You guys are still in school?"

"Not us, Josh," Bill says, and that's when I decide it's not so much that I dislike this guy as I actually kind of hate him. It's Tosh. *Tosh.* Four letters—how hard can it be?

Bill points to one of the windows. "That over there's a school. If they hear us playing, they'll call the oinks and that'll be the end of the Prophets as we know it."

Eek gives me a knowing nod. "But only in the sense that we'd have to find a new rehearsal space," he says.

"Which is hard," Bill adds, his pointless breath fouling up the air around us, "because, as I said, cheap space is impossible to find."

I nod like I get it even though I'm massive confused, and that's when Ravyn finally breaks her silence. She struts past me, reaching out with one long finger and running it across my chest as she passes.

"There are lots of abandoned buildings in this town," she says, only the way she says it sounds like a total come-on. I swing my messenger bag around in front of me.

Ravyn is halfway out of the room by then. She throws her chin over her shoulder, looks back in my direction.

"Coming?" she says.

Holy shit.

I double step it until I'm at her side. Three sets of muted footsteps fall in behind us.

As we duck under a length of low-hanging metal pipe, one of the guys asks Haze, "So, what's with the gas mask, sport?"

"It's for all the fucking asbestos in here," Haze says, and that's when it hits me. It's eight a.m. and Haze is still uncaffeinated.

Oh yeah. Shit's about to get real.

– 10.5 –

Ravyn is as sexy as any UnderWorld hostage I've ever seen. Taller than me by a good four inches, with dangerous curves and a slender waistline. And while one of the mission objectives of UpRising is to free as many hostage babes as possible, if this girl's supposed to be helpless, she sure doesn't seem like it. I've never seen any hostage in the Boneyard who's this fearless, this in control of herself.

Plus she's with a brigade.

Even so. I'd pretty much do anything for this girl.

- 11 -

We make our way through the eerie hallways of the hotel, lit only at the far ends by daylight coming in through broken windows. The ceiling is a mosaic of molded tiles, and even in the dimness, I can tell that the entire length of the corridor is covered in peeling paint and/or wallpaper.

"This is Peacock Alley," Ravyn tells me with a wicked smile that shoots my pulse into orbit.

"Why's it called that?" I ask. I have to say something, otherwise that word is just going to echo down the hallway for all of eternity with no resolution.

"It's because of the ceiling. It used to be colorful, like a—"

"Here," Bill cuts in. "Let's take 'em in here."

I want to drop max damage on Bill, and not just because he interrupted Ravyn before she could say "peacock" again. Bill's one of those douchey guys, like Psychobatter, who gets a little power and thinks he's a leet when he's really a total fail.

I watch the way Bill's mangled-feather hair bobs down the hallway, turns, passes through the doorway, and my core temp drops to absolute zero. Flashes of Goofy Golf flicker in my mind as everything around me skitters into slo-mo, and I can see it all: the go-kart track, Haze's drink cup, the blackbird dive-bombing our buggy. Whoever sent that bird into the game, it was the catalyst for everything. Bill's mangled-crow hair sends the shiver of thought through me that maybe we've made a tactical mistake by coming here. Maybe we've been lured into some kind of UnderWorld trap—I've seen it happen a billion times in the Boneyard.

We pass through a pair of double doors in which Castle-crashers have surprisingly left some glass intact, and swing into a room unlike any I've ever seen.

It's not so much a room as a hall, really—a huge, white-washed hall. The floor, the ceiling, the walls, the overturned piano lying on its side at the far end, all shrouded in decades-old layers of white dust. Everything except for the decorative molding, accent lines of dark wood that look like someone has outlined every possible point of entry. Or exit.

"This is our favorite rehearsal space," Ravyn says, the words floating in my direction like dust motes. "It's got good musical chi."

I want this girl so bad, it's not even funny.

"*Chi?*" Haze shreds the word.

"C-H-I," Bill says, and I've never wanted to hurt a guy so badly in my entire life since Stan. I want to take my shoe and smash Bill with it till he's nothing but yellow gut paint on the wall.

Apparently, Haze feels the same way.

"I know what you said," he hisses. "I'm not an idiot."

"Chi energy is like the breath of the universe," Ravyn murmurs from right behind me, her words brushing against my ear like she's telling me a secret.

I watch her, awed by the way she swirls around me like fog, how she rolls toward the windows, how she floats into a turn, bolts her smoky gaze onto mine, fans her fingers through her hair, smiles with every part of her face except her mouth.

Yeah. I could legitimately be in love with this girl.

And then she starts singing, and her voice carries into the open space of the room, and in spite of all the broken windows and debris, or maybe because of it, the acoustics are immaculate. Eek joins in and his harmonies are flawless. I focus on the words, something about transmutation, about ending up somewhere different from where you are, and this huge knot starts forming in my throat like when I was a kid and something bad would happen and I'd try like hell not to cry in front of the old man so he wouldn't give me crap for being a wuss supreme, and I'd end up having to go to my room and cry all alone.

just another turn . . .

not the whole road . . .

I'm sucking in air. All this dust. I can't breathe.

My mom would take me for rides in the car. Park it away from traffic and lights. Let me sob as hard as I wanted to. Sometimes she'd sob with me.

I turn away, swallow a throbbing mass of sadness into my stomach, but it's too big, it's too dense, it just wants to come back up again.

I don't . . .

I can't . . .

"Listen," Haze says as if he can read my mind. "This is cute and all, but Tosh and I have shit to do."

I try to pull in a deep breath, turn away from the window. "Yeah," I say. "We've got all this, y'know, shit we need to do."

Ravyn comes over, takes me by the hand. "Wanna see something cool?" she halfway whispers.

The tears shudder out of my body, as if she's performed a ritual exorcism by asking that one simple question.

All I can think is: *Please, yes.* Anything to make the noise go away.

I nod my answer, pushing back against the song and the sadness and all the shit Haze and I supposedly need to do, at least for now.

"We'll be right back," she says as she leads me by the hand, and against the best of my judgment, I follow her crazy, mangled-feather hair out of the room.

I don't utter a word as we pick our way through the silent corridors, past the paint curling off the walls, back down Peacock Alley (*say it again*, I silently beg), and up a few sets of crumbling stairs. Then another quick trek down a corridor, where Ravyn throws open the door to one of the rooms, and for a split second my hopes go airborne.

She motions me in.

There's a rotting couch in the room and not much else if you don't count the piles of debris. I desperately want to sit on those ratty cushions with her. I want to feel the grit of her dusty hair on my fingertips, the slope and curve of her breasts, her waist, the chalky smoothness of her skin. I want to kiss away the traces of coffee and sadness on her lips, taste the music still shimmering on her tongue.

Ravyn's definitely not the hostage here; if anything, I am. As if I could ever save this girl.

"Look," she says, lifting a hand to point. There's something weirdly familiar about the gesture.

But I turn anyway, follow the line of her finger out the decaying window frame, where the city skyline rises hazy and vague in the distance.

"Isn't that fucking cool?" she says.

I turn to her, and something happens to me that I can't explain, because I've only ever worshipped girls from afar and never in one trillion years would I talk directly to a girl I liked, especially if I thought she was hot. But for some reason my mouth opens up and before I know what I'm doing, I say:

"*You're* fucking cool."

She smiles but doesn't come toward me, and I'm not even the slightest bit thrown, because if at some point she lets me kiss her, it would be totally worth making that first move myself.

I take a step, and then another, and before I know it, I'm less than an inch away from her in front of what used to be a window. The breeze coming in through the opening carries a slight chill with it, and she doesn't stop me as I slip my hands around her waist, as I hook my fingers into her belt loops, as I lean in close enough to smell the cherry ChapStick coming off her lips. All we need is a microburst of kinetic energy and—

Ravyn lets out a little gasp, which I interpret to mean I'm about to stick the landing.

Incorrectly, I might add.

"Look," she says, reaching toward me. "You've got a side-kick."

She touches my shoulder, pulls back, and then—

There.

In her hand.

Is a cockroach.

Ravyn just plucked a cockroach off my fucking shoulder.

I try telling myself that passing out in front of the hottest girl in the Boneyard will not be a turn-on for her in the slightest.

That shrieking like a terrified three-year-old is not a manly thing to do.

That if I run out of the room, I'll probably end up falling through the decomposing stairwell and end up one floor down with a concussion—or worse.

"He's kind of cute," she says, holding it up near her face. She pets its long, flat exoskeleton with the tip of her finger. "Should we name it?"

Suddenly, kissing her holds far less appeal than it did less than a minute ago.

"I'm not a fan," is all I can manage to say as the urge to vomit roils in my intestines.

Ravyn looks up at me. "You should be," she says. "Cockroaches are really amazing creatures."

This can't be happening.

"I'm familiar with their many attributes," I tell her, damn near choking on the words.

She stares at me for a long, intense moment before setting the vile thing on what's left of the windowsill.

"They're symbolic, don't you think?"

"No." The word comes out of me too fast, hits too hard.

"The indestructible exoskeleton. The almost transcendental will to live."

But all I can think about is how to get out of that room the fastest way possible.

She steps forward. "Why the rush?" she asks as if she knows, as if she senses.

"Haze and I. We have some shit to do."

"Are you on a mission, Caleb Tosh?"

I never told her my name. Haze sure as hell didn't say it. Not my full—

"It's just, we don't have time right now because we—"

"Time spent unwisely waters the seeds of regret," she whispers, almost to herself.

My skin pulls into a full-body pucker. The text. On the subway.

Time unused melts into pools of regret.

I narrow my eyes at her. "What did you say?"

Her gaze drifts out the window.

"Regret is the shadow cast over a life that's been wasted," she murmurs, staring blankly across at the skyline. "Eek wrote those lyrics."

"Who are you?" I ask.

Ravyn doesn't respond, doesn't budge, doesn't even seem to breathe for a minute.

"Am I here to save you?" I press. "Or are you here to save *me*?"

"No one can save you," she finally says.

I feel my skin peeling, ripping down the length of my body. This girl's a Prophet. And she's telling me no one can save me.

"Then what's the fucking point?" I ask, rubbing the sting of dust or whatever out of my eyes.

But again she doesn't answer; instead I follow her line of vision out the window, wondering what could possibly have her attention in such a headlock. All I see is the brown-gray cityscape unfurling into the distance.

She swings toward me. "Aren't you going to answer that?" she asks.

I stare at her for an extra-long second, lock my sights on her as I slip the phone out of my pocket. How did she know? I never heard it go off, never even felt a buzz. I turn away just long enough to pull up the message.

It's a picture of a building.

That's it. No info, no address, nothing.

"Hey," I say, turning to hold the screen up where she can see it. "Does this look—"

I stop midquestion, spin a confused circle, panic-scan every square inch of the room. Then I bolt out into the hallway, where my worst fear is confirmed.

Ravyn is gone.

- 12 -

I've just barely processed that I'm standing alone in an abandoned hotel room when Haze's spooked voice calls up to me.

"Tosh! *Tosh!*"

I dash toward the sound, practically colliding with him in one of the stairwells.

"Dude," he says, panting to catch his breath. "I was explaining the physics behind those sick acoustics in the ballroom, and—"

"They're gone," I say.

He stares up at me, and I can hear his breath hit hard against the filtered chambers of his mask. "Exactly. Like . . . poof."

We stand in the stairwell, dust particles bigger than my whole head floating all around us. Haze is probably right. It's probably full of toxins and asbestos, and by the time we get back to Sandusky, I'll be riddled with lung cancer.

By the time we get back to Sandusky . . . The old man took off without saying where. Brought Devin with him. I don't know why he'd do that. Why he wouldn't realize I'd think the worst. That people who leave Sandusky tend to not come back.

The phone rattles in my grip. I pull up the message.

Time unused melts into pools of regret.

And just behind it, the same picture that came through a few minutes earlier. I show it to Haze.

"Do you know what this is?"

He takes the phone from me, looks at the picture, starts tapping the screen—pretty bold moves for a guy who essentially has no idea how a cell phone works.

"There's a link on the page to a bunch of other pictures," he says.

My face twitches in disbelief. Haze just used a techie word in a sentence. *Correctly.*

I take the phone from him, scroll manically through the photos. There's got to be a close-up view here or a link to a map . . . something. Why would the commandos direct me to a specific location on the map without helping me figure out what or where it is?

I'm scrolling at a good clip, not knowing exactly what I'm looking for, but confident that I'll know it when I see it. Sure enough, about sixty pictures in, one photo leaps off the screen at me in full-tilt 3D, and for a split second my knees buckle. Slack-jawed, I rotate the phone in my hand so I can study it from every angle.

High on a wall, surrounded by layers of cracked and curling paint, a clock stands frozen in time at ten minutes to four. The clock face is warped, some of the numbers twisted out of shape or gone completely.

It's melted.

The clock is melted.

Time unused melts into pools of regret.

Haze nudges me. "You're talking to yourself again. Why do you keep saying that?"

"Saying what?"

"Something about melting time? What's that supposed to mean?"

I show him the photo.

"So, do an image search for *melted clock*," he says.

His out-of-nowhere knowledge of cyber-sleuthing trips me yet again. "I gotta hand it to you, man," I say. "You may be off the grid, but you've got the mind of a brilliant lunatic."

He thanks me with a two-fingered salute as I start scrolling down the too-long list.

"Here," I say, getting a hit.

I click the link, and my hand falls limp to my side.

"Gimme a break," I whisper.

"What's wrong?"

"It's a *school*," I say. "Are you *serious*?"

"So it's a school," he says. "So what?"

So, a school has nothing to do with this mission. So, until we got to this hotel, I'd never even heard of a school in the Boneyard. So, I don't want to tell him that this is just one more dead end, like the ones in the tunnels that belch soldiers out onto the highway in flames.

But I don't say any of that to Haze. I can't. I just hand him the phone so he can see for himself.

Haze starts scrolling through the photos the same way he channel surfs at my house: torturously slow. He stops and studies every single picture before going on to the next; meanwhile, we're cramped inside that dusty stairwell, breathing asbestos particles the size of small cars. Well, *I* am, anyway.

"These aren't all pictures of that school," he finally says, pushing the phone back to me. "Look."

I have to confess here: I pull a Haze, start scrolling through the photos nice and slow. He's right. Some are pictures of old banks, old theaters, old schools, old hotels, old churches, even this hotel we're in, the Castle, all with one thing in common: they're all abandoned. Not just abandoned, but deteriorated, some to the point of complete and total demolition.

A fresh wave of fear crashes against me.

"Ravyn found a cockroach on my shoulder," I blurt out.

He snorts. "Well, isn't *that* symbolic."

"What do you mean?" I ask. Ravyn had said the same thing.

"You know. Your mom. Stan. The whole trailer infestation thing . . . Of course it would be symbolic."

The stairway flickers, and I hear the mantel clock *tick-tick-tick*ing like we're about to be ambushed, like we're about to wipe.

Where the hell are the commandos, anyway? When are they going to chime in, send me a brigade, something?

Haze is staring at me.

"That's crap," I tell him, the words sticking to the insides of my mouth.

But Haze's stupid glasses mirror my bullshit face back to me. "You know what I'm talking about," he says soft and low. "You wouldn't even leave the house until—"

"Wouldja shut up about that already?" I say, instantly regretting the harsh.

The last thing I need is a lecture on ancient history, though. I mean, that's not why he's here. I brought him along to help me stay focused on the now. Isn't that what he always says? *Be in the moment, live in the now?* Well, I need him *now*, that's for damn sure, and it won't help this mission if he keeps digging up what's already dead and buried.

We sit quietly in the stairwell for a while longer, until Haze, pragmatist that he is, says, "So, what do you want to do now?"

I look up, blink the sting out of my eyes a few times. Dust and asbestos everywhere.

"Let's eat," I say.

– 12.5 –

The two fried eggs on my plate look unmistakably breastlike.
I think about Ravyn and how, if that stupid cockroach would
have stayed the hell out of things, I might have had a chance to
touch hers.

– 13 –

This drippy, messy breakfast is the best thing I've ever eaten. Eggs swimming in an inch of oil, hash browns leeching grease next to them, bacon with little pools of melted fat in the curves of delicious porkness—even the pop is fantastic. I didn't realize how starving I was until the blue-haired waitress set these plates in front of us.

Haze and I don't talk for at least five minutes, don't utter a syllable unless you count our grunts and moans of gastronomic pleasure. When it finally registers that the tank is getting full, we slow down, actually chew instead of inhale.

I lean back, slide the napkin out from underneath the plate, mop my chin with it. Generally speaking, the Tosh men are napkin averse; the old man lets Devin's food dribble down the side of his mouth instead of wiping it for him, not caring if it stays there until the next meal or even the next day. I usually quick clean him up when the fat bastard goes into the kitchen for seconds, or thirds, or more beer.

But this food is so trashtastic, the napkin is a given.

Haze lets out a long, bacon-scented sigh and stretches his legs so far under the table, I have to move mine out of the way. He scratches his head through his split-pea-soup-colored beanie.

"The Prophets," he says. "How can you even have techno and folk together? It's self-canceling."

"Exactly." I slurp the end of my pop. "But I mean . . . they were there, weren't they? Because the next thing you know—"

"I know. Gone."

The word echoes inside me with nothing for it to land on. No soft place, no hard place, no safe place.

Gone. As in, nowhere to be. As in, doesn't exist.

How do you even begin to process 'doesn't exist' . . . ?

I throw the piece of toast I'm nibbling back onto the plate. The last bite won't go down, even with gulps of water.

I feel restless. Antsy.

"So, what are you gonna do about the school?" Haze says as if he can read my mind.

I let my gaze drift out the window and down the street, turn up the volume on the music coming into my ear so I don't have to hear the *tick-tick-ticking* of the invisible clock lodged somewhere in my brain.

Time unused melts into pools of regret.

I flip back toward Haze with a spark of epiphany.

turn back time

That's what her note said.

A locator app I downloaded one time sits unused on my last wall screen page. Supposedly, it spews all kinds of information about a place just by uploading a picture of it. I bring up the search window again, look for the name of the school since I'm pretty sure that's where the clock will be. *Industrial Tech*, it finally says. I can use the app to verify it when we get there.

"We gotta roll," I say, grabbing my bag and sliding out of the booth.

Since he's the one with the job, Haze is also the one packing money, so I let him pay for our food. The blue-haired waitress smacks her orange-tinted lips, watching us with mild interest as we wander out onto the sidewalk. Haze follows me silently down the sepia-toned streets of the city.

Before long, we come to a stop in front of what looks like a stone fortress at least half a dozen stories high. As I open the locator app, my pulse goes supernova with heightened awareness that we may have just been lured right into an ambush situation. Without any distinguishing markings on the building, I have no way of knowing if this is a minion fortress or an UpperWorld stronghold or something else completely.

Either way, it looks vacant.

I quick snap a picture, press a couple of buttons, and wait.

Industrial Technical High School.

Verified. But I'm feeling only a little calmer. I won't know for sure until I see the clock.

"We're going in," I tell Haze.

He motions toward the slick glass-and-steel building next door, whose backlit sign also reads INDUSTRIAL TECH.

"If you haven't noticed," he says, "school's in session."

"In a completely separate building."

"*This* building is wedged between a fully occupied school and a busy highway, Tosh."

"Where's your spirit of adventure?" I ask, scanning the perimeter for a point of entry.

"Where's your sense of reason?" he counters.

Haze doesn't seem to understand that sometimes in battle, it's necessary to take the full risk. To go max red, if need be. But why would he? I've never told him how any of this works.

"We need to stop a minute and think this through," he says.

"C'mon, Haze. When did you turn into a wuss?"

"When did *you* turn into Roundhouse?"

My eyebrows push up over the tops of the yellow goggles. I'd no more expect the word "Roundhouse" to come out of him than words like "links" or "Boneyard." Besides, Haze doesn't even own a TV. In fact, the only time he ever watches TV is at my house, and then he usually makes me put on the news or, worse yet, the History Channel.

I decide to test him.

"I bet Roundhouse would phone in a bomb threat or something," I say. "Get the school evacuated, create a massive diversion;

and while everyone's attention is focused on protecting their new state-of-the-art investment, we could slip in here completely unnoticed and do what we need to do."

I fully expect him to ask what it is we need to do. But he doesn't.

Instead his mouth gapes open. "You're not thinking about calling in a bomb threat, are you?"

The panic in his voice wavers in the air between us as alarm bells start going off for real over at the glass-and-steel version of I-Tech.

His head snaps in my direction.

"Phone's totally in my pocket," I say, lifting up both hands so he can see them.

He stares me down like he doesn't believe me, but really I'm just as surprised as he is.

"Dammit, Tosh—"

"I swear. I had nothing to do with it."

His eyes narrow at me.

"I swear to *God*," I add, because it's the only leg I have to stand on. "I didn't do anything."

Even so, all the little techies start rushing obediently through the glassed-in hallways and bleeding out the see-through doors of the überswanky Industrial Tech High School, and I watch with relief as they're ushered around to the far side of the building.

The other side. *Of course.* Our opening's around the back.

In which case, we don't even need a diversion, I tell myself, as we make our way around the fortress. The doors are bricked up, but I know there's a way in. No chance that raiders have left a place like this alone. Besides, it's too trashed for there not to be a hidden entrance somewhere.

Haze's muffled footsteps fall in behind mine like we're a couple of covert ops.

"You'd better be right about this," he says.

I'm thinking the same thing, but it would probably freak him out if I said so.

Behind the building, I scout for anything that screams on-ramp: door, window, knocked-out bricks. I finally spot it—there, closer to the end than the middle, is a crawl space barely big enough for either of us to fit through. A metal grate that's meant to cover the opening has been pried away, leaving a gaping hole that's the obvious point of entry.

I swing my bag over my back, wedge through the opening and into a dark crawl space, trying not to think about what else might be lurking down here. This time, unlike in the subway, Haze doesn't bring up ten-pound rodents or foot-long cockroaches.

We reach the end of the crawlway, where the space opens up and light pours in from broken windows. As my eyes adjust, I see that it's high enough for us to stand all the way up.

The alarm bells from the new I-Tech that still pierce through the midday air are now dulled by the layers of brick and concrete surrounding us.

We make our way inside, pick silently through the chaos of dirt, peeling paint, scattered debris, and broken glass. The stench of panic and fear overpowers the cramped area, bleeds into the thick air around us, kicks my pulse into fight-or-flight alert.

Our footsteps echo flat and dull through the long hallways. I stop at each classroom door, scan the walls for the melted clock, continue through the gauntlet of abandoned rooms, overturned desks, charred Bunsen burners sitting out on lab tables, broken pencils, papers plastered to the floor, undisturbed layers of dust and silt covering everything in sight. Someone has scrawled SAVE I-TECH in blue spray paint across a row of lockers.

Every now and then, I peer out a window, catch a glimpse of the cc's down below as they scramble around the new school, looking for the source of the alarms. Is this the work of the commandos? Is this their way of making sure I find the clock? Because when I do, I hope they'll solidify the rest of the mission for me.

"So what's your fascination with that clock, anyway?" Haze wheezes behind me as I poke into room after room to quick survey the walls.

I wish I knew what to tell him as I stop in front of a random doorway, stare into the stripped-bare classroom—white paint peeling off the walls, study papers strewn across the floor, a broken fluorescent light dangling from the ceiling by a single wire.

But the desks . . .

The desks are frozen in time, arranged in rows that are precision straight in a space that's eerily tidy. I don't need to look to know it isn't here. Not in this near-perfectly preserved room.

I back away, unable to find the words to explain to Haze what my fascination with the clock is.

That it's because I can still hear it.

Because it hasn't stopped ticking since she left, that's why.

Because my survival bar is flashing "the end is near" in glowing green letters, and I don't know how much time I have or how long I get to make things right this time. To level, to unlock some of those savory weps from the expansion pack so I can do something right for once. To become Worthy.

Because what kind of supreme fail would I be if I couldn't undo what I've done?

The noise from the crowd outside begins its slow ascent, climbing the walls of the fortress, winding through the broken windowpanes until it drowns out even the Motor City pumping into my left ear. I turn, disoriented, dart to a window on the other side of the hallway, only to find myself looking into a courtyard instead of down onto the area between the two schools. The students are streaming over from their designated safe side.

Holy shit. *It's some kind of mob.*

I start panic-dodging through one room after another. I don't even care which platoon it is at this point. I just want to find an exit so I can get downstairs and join this raid.

Haze follows close behind me.

"Tosh," he calls out. *"Tosh. What are you doing?"*

His voice syncs to the lyrics of the Motor City tune pounding in my head as I scramble in and out of doorways, looking for an exit. There must be an exit—this is a school, for Christ's sake. Correction: *was* a school.

You like shows about construction, don'tcha, Dev? The sound of my own voice reverbs inside my head as the picture flashes between Devin before the accident and Devin after.

Old I-Tech/new I-Tech.

Sometimes they put dynamite inside and blow the buildings up. You like that, right, Devin?

The hallway twists and bucks so violently around me, I have to stop in a doorway to steady myself. I slide my gaze up the far wall, lock sights on the clock.

The clock.

Hanging there, suspended in time at ten minutes to four.

The yellow goggles show in super-high-definition the way the outside casing is in pristine condition while the plate inside with the numbers printed on it has literally melted over the hands.

I tip my head, tighten my red-rimmed gaze.

Fire . . .

My palms smash against the goggle lenses. I clamp my eyes shut, but I can't block out the sight of the tunnel raiders pouring onto the abandoned highway, fully engulfed.

The heat of invisible flames coils around me, crackle-pops against my skin. The stench of burning flesh unbolts me from the spot, and I start shouting at Haze.

"*Get 'em out of there! Get 'em out of there!*"

But Haze just stands there, frozen in confusion, watching me scramble for an exit.

I don't blame him. He doesn't know the rules of the Boneyard because I never bothered to tell him. And now I don't have time.

I need to get down there, join the platoon, save the raiders, reach Turk's lair. I have to fix this.

Haze blocks my path. "Tosh," he says, his voice the softest, quietest thing in this abandoned building. "This isn't right. You're not right."

Wisps of charred debris float past me, stick to the sweat film covering my face as I back away from him, as I spin around, try to get some traction down the hallway.

Just as I reach the stairwell, the alarm clock on my phone goes off, even though I don't remember setting it. But I stop anyway, pull up the screen. Neon-green numbers pulse the time at me.

Ten minutes to four.

I stumble down the stairs as a huge disturbance erupts from ground level. The hordes of raiders are swarming toward us, shouting, waving signs and banners with the same two words scrawled across them.

SAVE IT!

"They pulled their own alarm," Haze says.

UpperWorld operatives, I tell myself. *Inside job.*

"They must've—"

He cuts his thought short.

Everything stops short, in fact: the sign waving, the marching, the cries of protest. Within seconds, the crowded space between both I-Tech schools has gone dead silent as a crane backs its way toward the mob.

A massive wrecking ball dangles from the top.

Seconds of absolute shock pass before the crowd catapults

into a deafening shouting match with a handful of balding comb-overs in brown suits planted stalwart next to the crane. The cohorts reek of smugness and apathy, and even though there's only a handful of them, their mere presence incites the mob's rage.

The riled-up crowd pushes forward again, gains momentum as it circles the wrecking-ball crane.

The brown suits are twitchy, nervous, not to mention ridiculously outnumbered and seemingly unprepared for a confrontation of this magnitude. Undaunted, they launch their own attack against the protestors by shouting counterthreats into a megaphone.

"Hey, where's your sign, man?" someone says, grabbing me by the arm and pulling me into the flow of the crowd.

I stammer like an ass-nugget, fully incapable of articulating a single coherent thought. There goes my invitation to join the raid.

"Are you deaf?" the kid says, putting a death squeeze on my scrawny bicep.

I throw a panicked look over my shoulder, spot Haze scrambling to catch up with me.

"I said, *where's your sign?*" The dude is maybe a year older than me, tall and ripped, with buzzed, nearly white hair dyed royal blue. Tenth Warriors often raid in blue battle gear. Is this guy Supershooter? I don't remember him being this much of a dickweed.

"I didn't make one," I say, trying not to stammer.

"No slackers allowed," he says. "We all agreed."

"I know, but dude, I'm here. I mean . . . I'm here, aren't I?"

He stares me down for a few seconds before letting me go with an unnecessary shove. It takes more than a few seconds for the blood flow to return to my arm.

"This is *important*, man," he says, brandishing his kielbasa-sized finger at me, and before I can respond, he's swept into the crowd again.

I survey the posse, the echo of royal blue in jackets, hair dye, face paint. Even the signs are painted in blue lettering.

I have no idea how many times we've circled the building so far, only that my ears haven't rung this bad since I went to that Metallica concert with Cam Tyler and his wannabe rock-star dad back in eighth grade, and no one said a word about how friggin' loud it was going to be, and I spent the next three days nodding vaguely at people without the slightest clue what they were saying.

The crane inches its way toward the school, and the energy from the crowd is reaching critical mass—any idiot can see that shit's about to get all the way real down here.

"We need to get lost," Haze hollers. He would think that, of course. He doesn't know. I should have told him how this thing worked a long time ago.

"We can't," I shout back. "We need to be here."

"Says who?"

Her note.

turn back time

"C'mon, Tosh. This isn't our fight, man."

The crowd surges forward, matching the bullhorns volume for volume, pushing closer to the suits and the school and the wrecking ball. We start to clot in the space between the crane and the old building, and before long we're toe-to-toe with the brown-suited comb-overs. The crowd around me is shouting so violently that tiny drops of spit occasionally hit my cheek, and I try to inch closer to the edge just to get out of the line of fire. As I toe the periphery, I see Supershooter standing there, only now the group has fully coagulated and the crush keeps me from moving away from him. My best strategy is to pretend one of us isn't there.

In the midst of all the screaming, a nearby cluster of blue-festooned Tenth Warriors spins a hushed conspiracy to commandeer the bullhorn and take control of the situation. As I spin around to eavesdrop, I'm almost taken out by a protest sign that reads THIS IS OUR FIGHT!

"We can't fail this," someone says into the cluster.

I fully understand the imperative.

"If we let them destroy this," Tenth Warriors whisper, "there are no second chances. Once it's gone, it's gone forever!"

The words ricochet against my ear along with a spray of frenzied saliva.

I throw a terrified glance over my shoulder, watch as Supershooter lunges for the bullhorn-toting suit, snags the device right out of the guy's twitchy hand, and comes straight at me. Before I can react, he shoves the bullhorn against my bony chest and says, "You wanna be part of this? Then say something, Einstein. And make it genius."

The raid.

I'm in.

Not to mention terrified, as the roiling crowd tumbles reluctantly into silence.

I frantically scan the crowd for Haze as Supershooter shoves me forward, and when I spot him, he gives me a nervous thumbs-up. For the record, I think he'd make a much better spokesman than I would. He's much more articulate, for one thing, not to mention incognito. But it's not his game, and besides, right now all eyes and ears are on me. The silence is brain-splitting.

The brown suits position themselves at my back, close in as tight as they can without actually touching me. I let my gaze slide up the side of the fortress, then down again, until it settles dust-like over the top of the crowd. I have no idea what to say as I lift the bullhorn to my face and hit the switch.

"The sky will fall."

My voice comes out the other end a hell of a lot stronger than it does going in. Not my words, I acknowledge. I'm stealing text messages someone sent to my phone. But still, my voice.

"And death will beat its wings against the ground."

I drop my arm for a moment, watch as the crowd murmurs and nods.

"The world beneath will weep blood."

The murmurs turn into loud whispers, and I feel my energy rising with theirs.

"And the known . . . will cease to exist."

Those last words come from nowhere, just roll out of my

mouth and into the crowd. The mob starts yelling and cheering and pumping their fists into the air, and suddenly a helicopter appears overhead with letters painted on the underbelly that I can't quite decipher. I swing around to the left and then to the right, as more and more bodies filter into the crowd, doubling the size of the mob in a matter of seconds.

Only these guys aren't Tenth Warriors.

They don't wear blue hair, or blue face paint, or blue anything.

They're infiltrators.

I drop the speaker, dash into the crowd, grab Haze by his coat sleeve. We fight our way through the crush of Tenth Warriors, half of which are climbing onto the crane, scaling the long arm toward the wrecking ball. The other half try to pick us up and crowd-surf us, but all I can think about is getting out of there before they realize that they've been hacked, that somehow UnderWorld minions are raiding their raid.

We sprint off campus and across a crowded overpass, not needing to stick around to know what's going to happen. All hell's about to break loose, and the abandoned building next to the highway is going to be demolished in the next few seconds. Concrete, glass, wood, dust, memories, dreams, gone—just like that.

I hope not too many of those raiders get taken out with it. That would hardly seem fair.

Then again, fair isn't in the playbook.

The thought shoots like a mortar round through my stomach.

I pull my phone out, thinking maybe I'll try the old man at home. He's gotta be back by now. He doesn't even go out drinking for more than a few hours at a time, and this time he took Devin with him. I don't really care what the old man does to himself, but the guy doesn't have the slightest idea how to take care of my brother.

When I unlock the screen, there's a message waiting.

From the cockroach.

Every bone in my body begins splintering under the weight of grim reality. . . .

I failed at saving the abandoned building.

I couldn't keep Tenth Warriors from the disastrous fate of incursion.

I'm an absolute fail.

- 13.5 -

We duck into a casino a couple of blocks away, where the cocktail waitresses have on these skimpy bikini tops that plunge so deep in front there's almost nothing left to fantasize about and microminis with lots of ruffles that make the skirts bob up and down as they wiggle through the casino, offering free drinks to the gamblers.

A girl in a neon-yellow wig sashays up to us, asks, "Can I get you handsome boys something to drink?"

I take in the heavy makeup, the starkly outlined cheeks and lips, the green-coated, black-rimmed lids, the heavy false lashes. When I get to her eyes, something about them makes me want to look away.

"No thanks," I tell her. "We've got shit we need to do."

- 14 -

We make our way to a bank of slot machines off to one side where there aren't too many people playing and hop onto the tall stools. I can't say it's quiet over here, but at least it's quieter than smack-dab in the middle of the casino.

"So what are we supposed to do now?" Haze says, not even trying to hide his irritation.

I take a slow spin, examine every square inch of this place. It's a decent hideout, at least until we can regroup, try to get some info, figure shit out.

I haven't even fully articulated a coherent thought before a buzz hits my back pocket. The last thing I want to see right now is Turk again, but I open it anyway, all judgment to the contrary.

The known will cease to exist.

By the time Haze notices, I've been staring at the screen so long I've lost the ability to blink.

"What's wrong?" he asks.

I clutch. I've never told Haze about the text messages. Not about Commandant Turk, who's been tracking me with my phone since before I started this rogue mission. Not about the commandos, who said I could be of use to them. And sure as hell not about the expansion pack—Haze would kill me for getting that invested after he warned me off the game.

Now, for the first time since we left Sandusky, I show him this one, since these exact words tumbled out of my mouth just minutes ago.

"Someone catches you on the news and is so inspired by what you said, he texts your own speech back to you. So what?"

I can't expect him to know it's from Turk when I've never told him about Turk.

I start nervous-swiveling on my stool, but Haze sticks his foot out and stops me midspin. "We're probably not even supposed to be here," he says. "The least you could do is not draw attention to that fact."

"Drinks, boys?"

The cocktail waitress has found us again. We turn to see her standing behind us in a classic supermodel pose (yes, the old man makes Devin watch that crap too—I usually switch it to *Roundhouse* whenever he leaves the room). She's carrying a drink in each hand.

"We're not gambling," Haze says, then quick backpedals so we don't get kicked out. He tries to drop his voice a whole octave. "Uh, not at the moment, anyway. We will be. Shortly. As soon as we decide on our best strategy."

I want to kick Haze under the chairs, but I know she'd see me.

"You're not gonna get very far on these slot machines, I'll tell you that much," she says. "They have 'em rigged so you have to feed it some serious coin before it'll kick anything back. And you can't walk away, because you're thinking, *One more slug and this baby's mine.*"

Haze pulls the edges of his cap down. "Yeah, well, we're a little light on slugs at the moment, so maybe we'll just—"

"Take the drinks anyway," she says with a fake pout. "They're terrible, but they're on the house."

Haze shakes his head, but I quickly relieve her of one of the cocktails.

She smiles as I sip what tastes like watered-down pop, then reaches into the pocket of her ruffled apron and pushes her hand toward me. I turn my palm up, and as she presses the object into it, I feel something pass between us, an electroshock wave of familiarity, of remembrance, of knowing. I lift up the bottom edge of the gaming goggles, but she's no less a vision in yellow without them.

"Have we met?" I ask, trying to get a better look at her under that masquerade of a getup she has on.

"That's the oldest pickup line in the book," she says, straightening her screaming-yellow wig.

Still, she winks at me before walking away.

"What'd she give you?" Haze asks.

I open my hand, look up in confusion.

It's a slot-machine coin.

"Why'd she do that?" he asks.

I shake my head, scan the garish, neon-lit casino, hoping to catch a glimpse of sunshine-yellow hair. It's a big floor, though, lots of banquettes with nooks and crannies that could swallow a person up whole.

I spin my chair back around, noticing the machine in front of me for the first time.

It's a slot machine called Hells Bells.

I look down at the coin in my hand, then back up at Haze.

get lucky, her note said.

"You gonna play it?" he says.

"I dunno. Should I?"

"What've we got to lose?"

I hand him the slug, which he immediately pushes into the machine, and then he pulls the handle. After a moment or two of jockeying for position, four sevens drop into place across the front of the screen. Bells and lights go off overhead, and for a split second I think it's because we're busted, but then I realize it's because we won. I expect the metallic *ka-ching* of dropping coins to follow, but it doesn't. Instead a small digital readout tells us how much we won and asks if we want to keep going.

Haze doesn't even consult me. He pulls again, and once again, a row of sevens rolls across the screen.

"Someone must've been on this machine all day and then gave up, like she said." He pulls the handle two more times. The first yields a win with sevens, the second with bars.

I kick a glance over my shoulder, jarred by the small cluster of brown suits taking casual strides in our direction. They're armed with sunglasses and antennae-like earpieces and who knows what else.

"Hey, time to cash out, man," I whisper. "I think we're about to get busted."

"One more," he says.

As my gaze nervous bounces over to the security minions, Haze pulls the lever again, only this time, it isn't a row of sevens that toggle into view, and it isn't a row of bars either.

It's a row of cockroaches.

"Jesus!" I shove against Haze's arm. "C'mon!"

He rips the printout from the machine, but as we turn to hop off our stools, it's obvious we're not going to get very far, because by now we're surrounded by a minuscule cc detail.

"It's best you gentlemen leave," one of them tells us in the deepest voice I've ever heard. "Now."

"I'll be sure they cash out and go," I hear from behind us, turning just in time to see that retina-piercing yellow wig push through the antennae and move toward us.

"Ready?" she says, sliding one of her slender arms through the crook of mine and the other through Haze's before guiding us toward the cashier cage.

"Just act like it's no big deal," she says once we're out of earshot, rushing us through the casino like the three of us just pulled off the heist of the century.

"Is this a holdup?" I blurt. I'm not sure why, except that she's the one who gave us that slug in the first place, and now she's escorting us with purpose to the cash-out window.

"You boys aren't eighteen, are you?" she asks.

Haze and I flash a worried glance at each other over her head.

"That's what I thought. Come on." She pushes us up to the cage, where a beefy dude with a shaved head bends down to greet us.

"Heya, Starlight," he says to her with a wink.

"Heya, Bubba," she says back, flashing him a thousand-dollar smile. "Can you cash these gents out? They lost track of time and just realized they have a ride to catch."

I wonder if she means that figuratively.

"Sure thing," Bubba says. As he studies our printout, I study the way he's oozing out of his casino-issue vest and how that dinky bow tie makes his fat head look even more mutantly huge. I wonder if they date, Bubba and Starlight. I wonder if Starlight is her real name or, you know, her *professional* name.

"They got this off sixteen hundred?" he asks.

Starlight answers with a musical, "Mmm-hmm."

"I thought sixteen hundred was off the grid."

"Guess they fixed it," she says.

"They sure as hell did." Bubba does not look happy. He glances up from the ticket, noticing me and Haze for the first time. "Which one o' you was on it?" he asks.

I don't waste a second sticking my thumb in Haze's direction. He sucker-punches me down low where Bubba can't see from inside the cage.

"Got some ID?"

My heart starts slam dancing but Haze just reaches into his pocket, cool as shit, and hands Bubba his ID card.

"And you're . . . Rutherford Hayes?" Bubba asks, his gaze ping-ponging between Haze and the card.

Rutherford? His name is Nate. Rutherford Hayes was a—

"When's your birthday?" Bubba asks.

That's easy. June 24, 1996, exactly two weeks before mine.

"May fourteenth," Haze says, "nineteen ninety-two."

He's lying, of course. I should know when the dude's birthday is. I've eaten Hostess cupcakes with him in my living room every year on that day since fourth grade. But here's my man Haze with a fake ID I've never seen before, spouting off his fake birthday like it's for real.

Bubba doesn't believe him. He leans over till he's halfway out of the cage.

"May fourteenth, you say?"

"That's right."

"What's your sign?" he says, and that's the moment I realize we're jacked. Totally and completely busted. Game over. Fail. Wipe.

"Taurus," Haze says.

My eyebrows lift over the tops of my yellow goggles, eyeballs pivot from Haze to Bubba. I'm awed as Bubba nods in satisfaction.

"Very well, Mr. Hayes. Two thousand sixty-four dollars and fifteen cents." He shakes his head. "Biggest payout I've ever seen on a coin slot machine. By about two thousand sixty dollars!" He tips his head back, hurls a sonic boom of a laugh into the air, then stops suddenly and lowers his eye beams at us one last time. "I'm calling maintenance to fix that goddamn machine."

"Okay," Starlight says. "Bye, Bubba!" She lifts a hand, graceful as all hell, and waves, and I get the strongest sense of déjà vu I've ever had. Is this girl a hostage? Have I seen her before, maybe tried to save her? I bet I tried, and failed, and now I'm getting another chance to free her. That's why I got the expansion pack. Extra chances to show I'm Worthy.

But I don't have time to linger on the thought. As Starlight leads us through the casino, she whispers, "Don't look back," only it's more like a stage whisper because of how noisy it is in there. But of course, the minute someone says don't do something, that's invariably the first thing you do. Haze and I both shoot a look over our shoulders, and I'll be damned if those buttoned-tight security ninjas aren't following a safe distance behind us.

"What do they want?" I ask.

"They might just wanna make sure you guys leave. The casino doesn't like it when someone cashes out big."

"That was hardly a big cash-out for a place like this," Haze says. "What do they really want?"

"What did Bubba mean by that machine being off the grid?" I cut in.

Haze turns on Starlight. "Did you do something illegal?" he demands, and I'd say his tone is starting to make me nervous except that I'm nervous as all hell already.

"Did *we* do something illegal?" I ask.

"Shut up, the both of you," she says, every ounce of sweetness evaporating from her words. "Just come with me, and for God's sake, quit asking questions for one single minute, would ya? I can't even hear myself think."

I avoid looking in Haze's direction, double-avoid telling him I think this girl's in trouble for real. He'll say *we're* in trouble too, and he'd be right of course; but if Starlight is a hostage, she's probably trying to escape, which definitely means we're here to free her.

My heart races at the thought.

Starlight's jaundiced wig and flouncy skirt aren't helping to keep us incognito as we push our way through the casino and out a set of doors that dumps out at some side street, not onto the busy avenue we entered from, like I was expecting.

We follow her into a multilevel parking garage, where she rushes up to a rimless sedan that might have been light purple at some point but is now just a vague shade of gray. That car looks rode hard and mistreated—a lot like its owner, I bet. My terrified heart begins to soften for Starlight once again. Unless, of course, she's about to clobber us and take the two large we just won—in which case my sympathy for her will lie dying next to me on the concrete floor of the garage.

"Get in," she says, and Haze freezes on the spot in a move so abrupt it would be comical if the whole thing wasn't so terrifying. "Get in!"

This time, Starlight's the one who sneaks a glance over her shoulder.

"Oh Jesus," she says, panicking now. "Get in or get left behind!" She scrambles behind the wheel, fumbles with the keys as Haze and I do a Three Stooges routine, trying to get ourselves into the car before the security detail catches up with us.

"I guess they didn't just want to escort us out," I say.

Starlight doesn't answer. She jams the car into gear and screeches out of the parking spot, leaving security behind in a puff of exhaust and terror. The tires squeal around every corner until we reach the exit of the parking garage, and without stopping or even looking, she hits the road, forcing the car that's already in our lane to swerve into the next lane to avoid a collision. The driver blasts his horn at us.

"Life or death, buddy!" Starlight shouts, flipping him the bird. I wish she'd pull her arm back inside before we incite the guy's road rage.

Haze is panting hard against his face mask.

"How is this life or death?" he asks, but she doesn't answer. She grips the wheel, eyes locked and loaded on the road ahead.

"Where are you taking us?" I ask.

"Me?" she says. "I'm not *taking* you anywhere."

Right. Cuz she's a hostage.

Haze's mouth twists into an almost-sneer. "You're seriously gonna tell us you're not taking us anywhere?"

"Then what are we doing here?" I ask.

She finally turns away from the windshield and flashes the most dazzling smile I've ever seen.

"How 'bout a trip to the park?" she says.

− 14.5 −

Starlight's real name turns out to be Starla Manley. She's eighteen—was only seventeen when she ran away from home with a guy named Scab, who dumped her as soon as they hit town. That, she says, is how she ended up broke and homeless and working at the casino. Of course, she had to lie about her age to get the job, but she says she had no choice.

As we merge onto the highway, she tells us she's done everything to survive, short of prostitution.

I wish she'd take that damn yellow wig off so I can see who she really is.

"**Why would you** tell us that?" Haze asks.

"Tell you what?"

"All that personal stuff. You don't even know us."

She kicks a stealth glance at Haze in the rearview mirror. "You seem like nice guys."

"Yeah. And, bonus, we're loaded."

A flicker of amusement crosses Starla's face, but it lasts only a nanosecond.

"I don't want your money," she says.

My eyes drift to her chest, to the rise and fall of each quick breath she takes. I want to appreciate the moment for what it is: the hotness of a girl's half-naked breasts pushing against the superlow cut of her blouse. But I can't. This girl's scared as hell and I know it.

I look away.

"Why'd you give me that coin?" I ask her, my breath flash-fogging the window.

"Why'd you take it?"

"I dunno."

"Yes, you do. Why are you so afraid of the truth?"

I shoot her a gritty look. "Hey, you don't know me. You don't know what I'm afraid of."

"I know you're afraid of cockroaches," she whispers, and the blood drains straight out of my face. I take out the phone, open the pulsing envelope icon I didn't even know was there.

Yeah. It's him.

"It's no mystery," she says as I try to blast the cockroach on my wall screen with hate rays. "I saw it on your face at the casino. That last spin on the machine—"

I swing on her. "Who are you?"

"I told you, I'm Starla."

"Fine. *Starla.* Why do *you* think I took that coin from you?"

"Same reason you came here to start with. You're hoping it'll do something for you that you can't do yourself."

"Is that right?" I practically spit.

"That's right, cowboy. You know how desperate people can get. You'd be amazed at what some folks are willing to do to save their own lives."

"That's pretty rich, coming from a girl who's running away from her—"

"Whoa." The tip of Haze's finger cuts right through the tension between me and Starla. "I hate to interrupt this witty banter, but look."

We all lean toward the windshield, staring into the distance, where, half a mile or so down the long, flat road ahead of us, the highway seems to just . . . end.

My face goes numb for a second or two. "What is that?"

Starla's mouth pulls into a one-sided smile. "That, my friends, is fog."

"We're from Ohio," I tell her, fighting to keep my voice steady. "We get fog. And I've never seen anything like *that* before."

Haze leans all the way forward. "Me either."

She turns, gives me the once-over, then Haze. She shakes her head.

"It's just weather, boys. Nothing to get crazy about."

But the closer we get, the more obvious it becomes—this is not your typical Midwest weather. This is biblical. It has all the appearances of a solid object, like concrete, like if we hit it at this speed, we'll bust into a million pieces of rust-worn car and human flesh. The memory ricochets through my entire body with a deafening gunfire report. Devin . . . the go-karts . . .

"Weird," Starla says.

"Ya think? Slow down," Haze tells her, and to my surprise, she does. She slows to a crawl just as we pass through, and not to sound overly dramatic or give the impression that I've watched too much stupid crap on TV, but it's a little like going through an interdimensional portal or something.

On the other side of the fog wall, we're instantly swallowed up. The road disappears, the dried grass off the sides of the road disappears, the other cars . . . We can't even see the hood of our *own* car anymore, much less a single fender of another.

"Whoa . . . ," Haze says, blowing the word through the chambers of his mask.

"We'll have to pull over till it passes," I tell her.

"No need. I've got lenses." She leans over, opens the wobbly glove box, pulls out what looks like a pair of gamer glasses identical to the ones I'm wearing. She puts them on, settles back, and breathes a contented sigh.

My hand shoots up to my face.

They're gone. The goggles are gone.

"Are you kidding me?" I swing back to look at Haze, but he just gives me a baffled shrug.

Starla is unruffled. "We get some pretty crazy fog around here. Not like this, mind you, but it's always pretty soupy."

"Where'd you get those?" I demand.

"From my father. He developed these lenses. They really work, too. Cuts the glare, makes it easier to see. Maybe you've caught the infomercials—they're usually on late at night." She kicks me a look, takes in my confused shock. "They're patented and everything," she adds, adjusting the frames against her face. "That's more like it," she says, then presses down on the gas until we're pushing forty, fifty, sixty, and beyond.

"Can I see them?" I ask, still a little lock-jawed.

"Not while I'm driving, potato chip."

The tiny little hairs on my arms prickle. I rotate, slow and cautious, to where I can see her whole face, and I'm hit by another supreme sense of déjà vu. My hand bolts toward her head, but before I can lay a finger on the goggles, *her* hand shoots out and grabs mine by the wrist. Damn, she's strong. And fast!

"Now, why on earth would you try something like that at a time like this?" she asks, cool as gazpacho.

"I'm positive we've met before." I jerk my chin over my shoulder. "Haze, doesn't she look—"

Skip it. Haze is out.

I spin the other way, press my face against the car window, squint hard. How can she see anything but fog out there, even with her so-called special lenses? The world outside is an ocean of white on white so dense, even the jet stream can be seen contorting inside the swirls of mist.

The known will cease to exist.

I swivel around again, slowly this time. Study her. Not her chest, not her wig, not her makeup, but her. Starla Manley, or whoever she is. Is she in trouble? Does she have any idea how right she was when she said this was a life-or-death situation?

"Why the sudden, desperate urge to escape?" I ask her.

"I could ask you the same thing," she shoots back.

The freezing subatomic particles of fog absorb into my skin, chill me to my cellular core.

Whatever. I don't even care anymore.

The phone buzzes in my hand. Hopefully it's the commandos, chiming in once and for all with some assistance.

It's Turk.

And my battery's going dead; the low light is winking in the corner of the screen. Great. Even my phone is stacking the odds against me.

"Do you have a cigarette lighter?" I ask.

She banks a look of skepticism in my direction, right through the lenses of the gamer glasses she jacked from me.

"You don't seem the type," she says. "Bad habit, though. You really should quit."

"I don't smoke. I just need to charge my phone."

"Oh. Sure. Let me light one up first, would ya?" She presses the lighter in and pulls a cigarette out of her apron pocket.

I fish my car charger out of my bag and plug it in when she's done, lean my head against the cool window and stare out. If you look close enough for long enough, you can see that the fog is made up of individual dots of supercondensed wet air. It's mind-boggling to consider how many dots surround us at this very second. Beyond trillions, beyond gazillions, whatever the biggest possible number is this side of infinity. There must be non-water-based particles floating around in the fog too: subatomic bits of what used to be something else, something tangible. Microscopic particles of decayed bird cells. Bits of departed souls. Things mixed up in the fog that were once real, that can't be seen or recognized anymore as anything remotely similar to what they once were.

The known will cease to exist.

I seriously hate this head noise.

"Can we turn on the radio or something?" I ask.

She doesn't answer, just reaches out and clicks the knob over. The way she keeps taking her eyes off the road makes me nervous.

"Let me do that," I say.

She leans back and lets me pick a station without arguing the point.

I turn the knob. Most of the stations are either fuzz or partial fuzz, and after going through the entire dial twice, I realize the only thing coming in clear enough to hear is talk radio.

If Haze were awake, he'd be in news-junky heaven, but instead he's passed out cold in the backseat. The sight of him lying there, inert, camouflaged in his knit cap and his glasses and his face mask leaves a life-sized dent in the middle of my chest.

A news break punches through the monotonous spew of chatter. Not that I'm even listening. I mean, the radio was just meant to be a filter for my brain noise anyway, but the words "I-Tech" jump through the speakers, and I quick hit the volume.

"A stay of execution was granted today for the building formerly housing the Industrial Tech High School."

"Hey," Starla chirps. "That's just down from the casino."

"Shhh."

"Demolition crews rolled into place this afternoon, only to find a protest in progress. An unidentified spokesperson rallied the mob to a fever pitch before disappearing into the crowd. His speech, however succinct, was enough to open talks between local officials and members of an underground coalition movement. In spite of a brief but volatile counterprotest, coalition members say their mission to prevent the destruction of the abandoned building was a success and has inspired them to take up the cause elsewhere."

A wash of relief pours over me, water-bucket style. I was invited to join that raid, maybe by Tenth Warriors and maybe by some other platoon, but I was tested, that's for damn sure. And I nailed it. Okay, so I failed the bird, but I nailed this mission. I'm well on my way now. This is going to rack up some serious Ascent Credits. I'll get a few more like this under my belt, but ultimately I'm going after Turk's lair. I can smell the victory as I unbuckle, lean over the back of the seat, wrangle Haze by the arm of his jacket to snap him out of his narcolepsy.

He grunts into semiconsciousness. "Wha—"

"Wake up!"

He shakes his head, scratches the back of his neck. "What for?"

"The old—dude, are you listening? We saved I-Tech, man. *We saved it.*"

Haze sits all the way up, looks around. "Where the hell are we?"

I slowly turn around, lower myself onto the seat, buckle up again.

"Yeah," I ask Starla. "Where are we?"

She smiles. "Xanadu, boys."

I no longer recognize the map we're on. Starla Manley is purposely taking us off course. Maybe she's not really a hostage; maybe she's a minion *cleverly disguised* as a hostage.

"Listen," I say, digging my heels into the floorboard. "It's been nice of you to give us a lift and everything, but . . . we really have no need to go to Canada."

"*Xanadu,*" she corrects me. "And you most definitely do."

"We really don't."

"We have shit to do." Haze mumbles what appears to be our new mantra from the backseat.

"Then tell me," she says—only the way it comes out sounds like a challenge. "Where do *you* think you need to go?"

Regrettably, I haven't unlocked that part of the mission yet.

"What's in Xanadu?" I ask, testing her.

"Home."

"Whose home?"

She smiles without looking at me, nods without answering.

"Whose home?" I ask again.

"You're a clever little monkey, aren't you?"

For the first time since we met her, Starla clams up, and the next few hours pass long and quiet. We let the drone of talk radio fill up the space inside the car. We stop for food, which Haze pays for. We stop for gas, which Haze pays for. Starla never offers, never thanks us; it's almost like she thinks *she's* the one doing *us* a favor.

We spend the night in the car in a parking lot somewhere, and in the morning the fog still has a choke hold on everything in sight. Buildings, trees, cars, people, all reduced to vague shapes and variegated shades of white and gray.

The known will cease to exist.

− 15.5 −

Starla Manley is not who she says she is.

– 16 –

I don't know how to prove it.

And maybe I'm just being paranoid, but I don't know what else to think of this girl. Sure, she *looks* like one of those self-consciously sexy UnderWorld hostages. I even thought that part of this mission was to rescue her. Now I don't know *what* to think.

Only that this girl is no more Starla Manley than I am.

With the fog pressing in on us from every angle, we roll into town, down street after street of limestone buildings that have all but disappeared in the thick, milky air. My mind drifts from the fog to the Castle to I-Tech as we push through miles of the same sameness.

I reach my hand into my bag, let the fringe of the blackbird feather slip against the tips of my fingers. I take it out, move it to my coat pocket.

The known will cease to exist.

I don't *hear* the words so much as *feel* them echo through the gaping emptiness inside my body. Devin. The go-kart track. Haze was there—he knows what it was like. I couldn't have stopped it if I'd wanted to. How was I supposed to know nothing would ever be the same after that?

The fog thins out some as we turn off the highway onto a single-lane road that's overgrown and weedy, past an old brick building with GOLD MEDAL FLOUR painted on the side, just barely visible through the mist. A rusty, tilted sign off the side of the road says ON-RAMP even though there's no highway in sight, then one more turn down a dirt path, followed by a long haul to the end of it, and the whole time, Starla doesn't utter a single word.

She finally stops in the middle of a crack-ridden parking lot, pulls the hand brake. Haze and I lean forward to get a better view.

"What's this?" he half whispers as we stare at the amusement park percolating in the fog before us. The spiraled bones of a roller coaster rising in the distance, the long-chained swings of Devin's favorite ride swaying against a phantom breeze. The chipped plastic face of a clown with a snow cone dangling by a single screw from the roof of a warped food hut. I always got blue coconut, even though the old man said it was a wuss flavor. He hailed Devin's choice of tiger's blood.

"I thought you said *park*," Haze adds, the words bathed in accusation.

Except, clearly, that's what this is.

The last time I saw this parking lot, it was packed with news vans. They're gone now. Mostly gone, anyway, except for a single burnt-out, rusted hull tipped over on its side at the far end of the lot.

One last, lone Airstream trailer sits just inside the entrance, right behind a bolted gate with no fence around it.

Inside the car, nobody moves.

"It's okay," Starla finally says. "Go." As I reach for the door handle, she snorts and adds, "It's not the end of the world, for God's sake."

The words flay the skin right off my bones.

The end is near.

I slow-mo my way out of the car and Haze stumbles out after me. We stand there, slack-armed and confused as all hell, until I hear Starla jam the car in reverse. I swing around just in time to see her blast off down the dirt road. She doesn't even shift gears before taking the turn onto the street, and as the little gray sedan disappears in a puff of dust and fog, I realize with a thousand volts of raw, electric horror that I just made the third-worst mistake of my life.

"Hey!" I scream. "Hey, *wait!*" I lunge down the road after her, chasing the car on foot and hurling an Uzi round of profanity the entire way.

Haze trots after me. "Tosh! What's wrong?"

How do I begin to articulate that Starla Manley has just left us stranded in the middle of nowhere . . . ?

And she took my phone with her.

I don't make it very far down the dirt road before I start wheezing in agony. I bend over, grab my thighs, catch my breath until I'm ready to launch again.

"Damn it all to hell!" I scream, kicking at the dead grass shriveled inside cracks of faded asphalt.

"*What's wrong?*"

I don't want to say it. I really don't. But I have to.

I brace myself.

"Starla's got my phone."

"*What?* You let her take it? Why'd you let her take it?"

"I didn't *let* her do anything, Haze. It was plugged in when she fled the scene. *Goddamn sonofabitch!*"

The door of the Airstream flies open and a wiry coat hanger of a man in a wheelchair rolls down a too-short wooden ramp, gaining momentum as he hits the bottom.

He spins the rear wheel with one hand and levels the barrel of a shotgun right at us with the other.

"I hope you boys know Jesus!" he calls out.

My arms fly up in surrender, like I did that day at Goofy Golf when I was surrounded by commandos. I start to back away, but it soon becomes obvious that there's no need to beg for our lives here. I drop my hands back down, stick them in my pockets, and nod at him, just once.

"You selling tickets today?" I ask.

Haze latches his stunned gaze onto me. I'd do the same in his position.

The old geezer sizes the two of us up without saying a word. For a second I think maybe he's fallen asleep. I keep my eyes on the gun, and as soon as the barrel flags just a bit, I take a step or two forward.

"Who are ya?" the geezer finally says, reanimating, using the gun to point at us in a way that makes me bead with sweat. "What d'ya want?"

"We want to buy some—"

"Y'don't look like much, neither of ya."

"No, I guess not," I say, eyeing the way his wilted body folds into the harsh angles of the wheelchair. A little backwash of stomach juice rises into my throat, and for a split second the old geezer goes in and out of sight, strobing alternate images of him and Devin in that chair. I swallow against the burn.

"We'd like to go in," I say. "Do we need tickets for that?"

The shriveled old carny dismisses the thought with a wave of his gun-wielding hand.

"No one come in here in years. Decades." He turns and spits, mumbles something unintelligible.

"Are you the only carny left?" I ask.

I can hear Haze's breath spinning through his filters.

The old guy lets his arm go limp, lets the barrel brush against the ground. "Others left after the accident," he says.

The air fills with distant, silent screams and the hollow sound of chopper blades. I clamp my eyes shut, wishing I had my phone, wishing I could drown out the noise.

Others left after the accident.

After the accident.

"So . . . the tickets?" I ask again, squeezing my face tight to keep the sting off it.

I look up just in time to catch his watery, hazel eyes follow the twisted, rusting skyline of the amusement park.

"This place." The rifle wobbles in his flimsy grip as he points it in the general direction of the park. "It don't sing anymore. Don't dance. People say it got no soul."

I squeeze my eyes so tight they burn. But I still see Devin. Curled up and useless. Swimming in his oversized wheelchair.

Haze's elbow catches me between two ribs. "Let's get the hell out of here."

"You watch your mouth," the old guy says, wiping spit off *his* mouth with the back of his hand. "It hears you. It knows your heart."

Haze turns his head away from the carny, lowers his voice to a whisper.

"This guy's a goddamn lunatic, Tosh."

"You boys need to quit talking about God like He ain't here," the old man says. "He's everywhere, an' don't you forget it! *The Lord Almighty will come with thunder and earthquake and great noise, with windstorm and tempest and flames of a devouring fire.*"

I hazard a few more slow steps toward the carny, my heart metal-thrashing a frantic rhythm inside me. "Can we go in?" I ask, hoping to snap him out of his incoherent tirade.

"*Thunder and earthquake!*" The old geezer starts pushing himself around the yard, his rickety wheelchair wheezing from the exertion. "*Tempest! And flames!*"

He doesn't even know we're here anymore. I grab Haze by the arm, push him past the locked gate with no fence around it as the carny shouts on, waving the rifle around for emphasis.

"The end *will* come! You'll see. You'll see, boy."

The words ring in my ears like gunshots.

I spin around. "What'd you say?"

But the old guy is rolling in circles, lost in his rant. *"Windstorm, and great noise!"*

Haze pushes me forward, and we stumble onto the amusement-park grounds. I run like I know where I'm going, like I've been here before. Which I have. I mean, I've been to Goofy Golf loads of times, only Goofy Golf doesn't *have* a roller coaster—you have to go to Cedar Point for that. Not that we ever did. The old man would never spring for us to go to a deluxe park like Cedar Point. Maybe if we'd gone *there* on my birthday instead—

I snap off the end of that thought, use the soaring track of the roller coaster as my beacon, spot the go-kart track up ahead. Buggies piled in a junk heap off to the side. Even so, I can almost hear the roar of the engines echo faint in my ears.

"Tosh, wait up," Haze says, and it's only then that I realize I'm running.

Running straight for the track, which is barricaded by chain-link. Nothing in my arsenal to cut through something like that.

Haze easily catches up to me, says nothing as I clutch at the fence till my fingers go numb. I stare at the bleached-out buggies stacked up against the concrete wall, exposed to time and the elements.

I'd give damn near anything for some Bunny Puke in my ear to drown out the phantom noises of the go-kart engines, the screams of people plunging down the steep arc of the now-crippled roller coaster, and the whispered echoes of carnies hawking corn dogs and cotton candy and funnel cakes.

I start pulling at the fence, hoping to find a weak spot, an opening, a section that's not clamp-fused to the rusted metal posts. I have to get in there. Have to go back, to fix it. To save it. It'll be different this time. This time I'll know exactly what to do—that's why I got the expansion pack, *ASCEND: Armageddon*. To get another chance at coming back to this level. To try it again.

I alternate tugging at the fence and grunting like a caged animal, but the sound is hollow and distant, like it's bouncing back at me from somewhere else.

"Tosh," Haze says. *"Tosh."*

I start to climb.

"What are you doing?"

I can't tell him the truth now—we're too far in it. I could never make Haze understand the simple appeal of the Boneyard: if you fail, you can always try again.

All I have to do is become Worthy.

As I tumble over the back side of the fence, I feel the blow-back from the go-karts whizzing past, even though I know these karts haven't been moved in years.

Winded from the climb, I bend down, quick catch my breath. I taste the ages-old exhaust fumes and remnants of deep-fried funk that seem to still hang in the fog after all this time as I suck in lungfuls of air.

I open my eyes, shoot my gaze straight at the dog pile of go-karts, mentally stripping away each buggy until I see the one at the bottom, the one beneath it all. Dim yellow paint chipped in sections, frame twisted up like it's cowering in fear.

Back tire spinning for no discernible reason.

"You boys wait up!"

I'm not sure how he made it so far so fast, but the carny's calling out from behind us.

"Hey! Stop right there!"

I turn in time to see the guy come jogging straight up to us, and my blood runs cold as I crane my head around, looking for a wheelchair that should be there but isn't. My vision short-circuits, flickering like when the cable goes out. For a split second I see news footage of the bird die-off down at Goofy Golf blinking in between the abandoned highway in the Boneyard and the carny, who's now headed our way.

I spin around, grab Haze by the arms, hoping I can see something in his lenses: a superimposed view of the map, maybe, or the reflection of a Medic in those mirrors, or any explanation for the massive heal that has turned the old geezer into a fucking soldier whose hulked-up body is *jogging*, not walking, toward us.

But all I see in the reflection of his cop shades is the Caleb Tosh who turned twelve at the Goofy Golf Amusement Park in Sandusky, Ohio, four years ago.

The young, sweat-stained carny is right over my shoulder.

"You need tickets for this!" he barks around a fat cigar.

"I know how we can sneak in," Haze says, and I turn my disbelieving eyes on his bare head: no shades, no beanie, no face mask. Just his dusty head of stiff kid hair, so dirty it doesn't even move as we spin off toward the tracks.

I go back to scanning the go-karts with an urgency I can't explain. They're all lined up now, a row of shiny, happy buggies just waiting for action. I recognize ours right off: the bright yellow two-seater, sitting at the front of the pack, chugging and ready to go.

"Hurry," Haze says, pushing up against me. "The carny!"

"Screw the carny!" I shout with glee.

"Shh! Don't let your mom hear."

My mom . . . ?

I swing around, recoil at the blast wave of "Surprise!" that hits me. About a dozen kids from school sit around a Goofy Golf picnic table with a plastic tablecloth covering it, festive paper plates scattered along both sides, and dozens of balloons and an ass-load of candy and punch and a big old sheet cake frosted in white with those brightly colored icing balloons that turn your whole mouth blue.

I look up. My old man's got a cigarette dangling out the side of his mouth, and next to him, my mom is standing stiff and tight, like someone shrink-wrapped her.

"What are we doing here?" I ask, gape-mouthed.

"It's your birthday, jackass," the old man says. "Don't go and do anything stupid."

"Come on," Haze says, pulling me by the sleeve. "Let's hit the go-karts."

Hey, yeah! Once a kid turns twelve, he can ride without a

grown-up. Haze and I have been waiting for this day our whole lives.

"Come on!" Haze calls out. "What's the holdup?"

"We're going to the go-karts!" I shout, and the posse of boys sitting at the table scrambles after us.

"Take your brother!" the old man bellows.

When we hit the tracks, Devin wants to ride with us.

"Get your own, ass-puke," I say, gloating over the fact that he's two years too young to get his own.

"But I wanna ride with you guys." He starts climbing into the bright yellow buggy with us.

"Buzz off!" I push my hand against his chest, against the thin fabric of his T-shirt, against the bright green background with the yellow Termi-Pest logo printed across the front.

COCKROACHES ARE OUR SPECIALTY.

Haze shoves me into the seat and climbs in over me. He takes the last few sips of pop and throws the cup out of the buggy as I fire it up, shooting down the tracks like a bat out of hell.

Devin gets into the kart behind us with a kid from my class who I hate so much I'm not even sure why he's at my party except that our moms somehow know each other.

I gun it.

"Slow down!" Haze calls to me, but I'm a newly minted twelve-year-old on a mission.

"Slow down!" he screams, pointing at a blackbird that's headed straight for us. "Watch out!"

I scream, jerk the wheel. Our go-kart slams into Devin's,

ricochets into the wall. Tire hits concrete, go-kart goes vertical, catches, flips over once, twice, tangles with Devin's.

In a flash, we're strewn across the track, the air around us thick with shrieking go-kart engines and cries of agonizing pain.

I open my eyes.

The doctor is setting my broken arm and I'm screaming bloody murder because it hurts like hell and my mom is folded into the corner of the room as the old man rants about how this is the fifth emergency-room visit we've made that year alone and how if Devin and I weren't such jackasses we wouldn't be in this position again, and I can't even sit next to her and comfort her because the next thing I know, this other doctor comes in and just blurts it out.

He will never walk again. He will never talk again.

Devin's body is an abandoned, empty hull.

I haven't even been twelve for a whole day.

The fog rolls in as the wheels of that faded yellow go-kart spin silently at the bottom of the heap.

Haze calls over to me as I lift myself out of a crouch, as I start walking, then running, down the go-kart track. I hear him jogging to catch up to me as I get to the third turn, where I fully expect to see a green-and-yellow drink cup with a mostly dead bird lying next to it.

But it isn't the bird I see below the skid mark, not moving, barely breathing.

It's Devin.

Crumpled on the concrete track inside his worn black hoodie.

Curled into an impossible-shaped heap.

The puniest of agonized moans leaking onto the concrete next to a thin stream of blood.

"Devin!"

Haze grabs my jacket as I lunge forward.

"Tosh! There's nothing there," he says as the blood and the hoodie and the Devin-shaped heap disintegrate into particles of fog, rise up in a sudden gust of wind, spin around us before dissipating into the agitated sky.

I hear the synchronized cadence of army boots, *the tick-tick-ticking* of the mantel clock, the thrash-pummeling of my own heart, slamming to break free inside my body.

I didn't fix it.

I'm not Worthy.

I can't Ascend.

− 16.5 −

If I had a mapper, maybe I could figure out where the hell I am.

– 17 –

I have serious concerns about how long I'm going to be able to walk since this is already the farthest I've walked in my entire life if you add up all the walking I've ever done. I don't even know where we're supposed to go now because I don't have my phone to guide me. No GPS. No locator app. No way to receive a message from the commandos, should they finally decide to freakin' send me one. This is dire. Like your-platoon-was-obliterated-in-a-raid dire. Like you're-losing-your-grip-on-the-entire-mission dire.

The girl standing next to a gas pump filling the tank of her Jeep is the first human being we see after leaving the amusement park.

Her T-shirt says SUPERGIRL—ironic, since she's a study in plainness: plain brown hair, plain blue eyes, 501s, black Chuck Taylors. She isn't wearing makeup, isn't smiling, doesn't even seem to notice the two of us slogging past, and Haze and I cut a pretty noteworthy image after the hell we've been through.

Whoever this girl is, I doubt she's super-anything.

We swing into the convenience-store part of the gas station to get a pop and have a whiz. I suggest stocking up on provisions since we don't know what's going to happen from here, but Haze doesn't want to, says he has nothing to carry provisions in. I grab a bag of snack mix off the rack and a couple of Mountain Dews out of the cooler, which he then has to pay for. He makes it seem like a gigantic pain in the ass to take his wallet out of his pocket, but he also refuses to let me handle any of the winnings from the casino.

"I can hold some of that money," I tell him, casting a look out the store's front window. Watching a wallpaper girl pump gas is still better than not watching any girl at all.

"If it wasn't for me," I remind him, "you wouldn't have won that money in the first place."

Haze's face goes from zero to rage in three-point-five seconds.

"If it wasn't for you?"

Whoops.

"You mean if it wasn't for you leaving your phone in Starla's car? Or if it wasn't for you breaking into that school, or that other building, or that subway station? If you hadn't stolen a car and wrecked it in the first place—is that what you mean? Man, if it wasn't for you, I wouldn't be dragging my ass through Bumfuck, Nowhere, with no way to get home. I have a chem test on Thursday, Tosh!"

The clerk snorts as he hands over the change.

I try to block his way out the double glass doors. "I just meant—"

"Don't talk to me right now," he says, brushing past me.

We leave the store, walk across the parking lot toward the road. I get a vague sense that Supergirl is tracking us in her sights, but I'm a thousand percent more worried that Haze is upset with me for losing our only connection to the UpperWorld—my phone. I have to figure out how to get through to him. I mean, I need the guy more than ever right now. It's not his fault that I ditched a perfectly good platoon back at I-Tech, but we were about to go under siege, and if I'd got caught, I'd be screwed ten ways to Sunday right now. But I'm in desperate need of platoon members, so like it or not, Haze is the only backup I've got.

"Hey," I call out, trying to think on my feet as he barrels down the road ahead of me. I need a hook. For me, a simple offer of junk food usually does it. Haze's weakness?

Random factoids.

"Yo, Haze. What was the carny shouting out back at the amusement park—do you know?"

"Revelations," he says. The word clips the air between us, but at least it's something.

"From the Bible?" I ask. "What does it mean?"

"I don't know, Tosh. Why don't you look it up on your phone? Oh, that's right. Because you don't *have* your phone. Because you left it in some girl's car."

"Hey! That wasn't my fault! The battery was almost dead—I had to charge it up. What was I supposed to do?"

"Try taking it *out* of the car before she strands us in the middle of nowhere."

"Do you really think I knew she was going to leave us there? How would I even know that?"

"You wouldn't, Tosh. You wouldn't know anything. I bet you don't even know what you're doing here."

"I'm on a mission!" The words are out of me before I can hit the kill switch, words I never wanted to say in front of Haze because he wouldn't understand. He doesn't know the Boneyard the way I do, doesn't know what's supposed to happen.

The look on his face solidifies my fears. Massive tactical error.

"A *mission?*"

I nod.

"You're on a mission?" He's breathing sweat and anger all over me, even from inside his mask. "To do what? Save the fucking world?"

I square myself in front of him, open my mouth to answer, only nothing comes out.

He throws his hands up.

"You know, I think I've been pretty patient, Tosh. I've stuck with you through all the shit times. Hell, I even went through some of those shit times with you. And I haven't said one word to you about any of this, but I can't make you want to be part of—" He stops, shakes his head.

"Go ahead," I tell him, glad that it's rage fuming through me and not tears. "Be part of what?"

"Whatever. Go on your little mission to save the world. I give up."

"Give up on *what?*"

"On trying to save *you!*" He's standing inches away from me, his words swarming me, crowding me with aggressive energy. This is not the attack I was expecting.

Am I here to save you, or are you here to save me?

No one can save you.

I shove against him with the flat of my hand.

He answers by shoving back.

We're just about to level up to a bona fide fight when the squeal of tires stops us both in our tracks. We spin around in time to see the Jeep pull up behind us, stand slack-mouthed as Supergirl gets out and slams the door behind her. We continue to stare at her as she approaches, and while I'm grateful to have our fight interrupted, I also wonder what this girl could possibly want with us.

"Glad I caught up with you," she says, jogging the last few steps. "You dropped this back at the gas station."

She's holding something in her outstretched hand, her fist wrapped so tightly around it that I can't tell what it is at first. She moves closer, unfurling her fingers, and it takes me a full minute to register what I'm looking at.

"Where'd you find that?" I ask, snatching my phone off her open palm.

"You dropped it at the gas station," she says.

I squint at her, hard. That's impossible. Unless . . . Could she be Starla, out of costume? I look again. Is it possible? It would have to be—how else would she have gotten my phone? But this girl bears zero resemblance to Starla Manley, and believe me, I'd know. I spent the entire time it took to drive from the cockroach casino to the dead amusement park staring at her, mentally stripping away all the makeup and the wig and the skimpy costume, so I'd at least recognize her smoking-hot body, if nothing else.

No, I can assert with absolute conviction: this girl is not Starla Manley.

"So you found this at the gas station?" I ask.

"Uh-huh."

"Really? Cuz I didn't have it on me at the gas station."

"Oh," she says. "Well, I found it on the ground after you guys left. I just assumed it was yours."

I peel my eyes away from her long enough to inspect the phone. It looks like mine. I unlock the passcode. The home screen looks right. All my apps seem to be there. But somehow I still can't believe it. There's only one way to be sure, though, and that's to pull up my messages. The commandos must want to talk to me by now, even if it's just to squawk at me for being such a lame-ass.

But they've sent nothing.

I glance up at her. "Starla?" I ask.

She slow-shakes her head in response, kicks me a look of pity tainted with suspicion.

"Anyway, is it yours? Because otherwise I'll take it back and have them put it in lost and found."

"No," I say, confused as all hell. "It's mine."

She shrugs. "Good. Glad that's settled."

Supergirl turns on the heel of her black hi-top Chucks and cruises back to her Jeep. I shoot a quick glance at my phone again and then back up at her just as she starts the engine.

"Hey!" I call out, jogging up to the driver's side door. "Can we catch a ride?"

"I don't think so," she says, putting the Jeep in reverse.

I did not see that one coming.

"Wait. Why not?"

"Forget it," Haze calls over. "Let's just walk."

"Walk *where?*" I shout. I didn't think he was listening, and besides, I haven't forgotten that we're in the middle of a fight.

"I don't care," he says, his voice hovering in the dead air around us. "Home. Let's just figure out how to get home."

I bite my lip to keep from telling him the truth about going home, that if I don't fix what's wrong, there's nothing to go home to. I want to explain it. I really should. But I can't get the words out. What is it about saying something out loud that makes it so final? You can't unsay words; they become particles floating inside fog along with all those subatomic microbits of dead birds and crashed cars and charred remains of things that used to be real and whole.

Besides, what happens if I tell him everything and I still can't fix it? For one thing, Haze will finally know what an epic loser his best friend is. That Caleb Tosh could not Ascend. Who'd ever stand by a fail like that?

Who'd want to stick around to watch a complete and total wipe?

The wind kicks up, tousles my hair just the way Devin used to do, just to annoy the shit out of me.

Haze turns, starts walking.

"Haze," I say.

"You suck, Tosh."

Supergirl leans out the window and says, "Man, you two are pathetic. Get in."

My gaze volleys between her and the good-bye side of Haze.

"Hey!" I yell. "We got a ride."

He doesn't stop, but slows down enough that I can tell he's thinking about it. I hoist myself into the passenger's seat.

"He'll get in if we pull up next to him," I tell her. "I may have to grovel a little, though."

"Then I guess you'd better buckle up," she says.

I hope she's not speaking metaphorically.

− 17.5 −

Her name is Mason Barshaw. She says she hails from Peculiar, Missouri, which is ironic since the only peculiar thing about her is her name.

And the fact that she's here.

Alone.

- 18 -

"**Where are you** headed?" Mason asks as Haze scrambles in behind the driver's seat.

"South," he says.

"So how come you were walking north?"

He keeps his mouth shut but skims a blistering look off me.

"No phone," I say before he cuts loose. "I guess we were turned around without our GPS."

"Hmm. Good thing I found it, then." She doesn't look especially relieved, though. She doesn't look especially anything. Mason Barshaw is a blank canvas.

She constantly checks her mirrors as she drives, and even though I myself am a novice at the wheel, I'm no stranger to the habits of paranoia.

"Where are *you* headed?" I ask.

"Don't exactly know yet."

My hair prickles.

"What exactly does that mean?"

She hits me with a look like she's trying to decide whether or not to answer, like she's sizing me and Haze up. I get the sense that the scale isn't tipping too well in our favor.

"Let's just say I'm on a mission," she says at last.

Haze sputters. "Intriguing."

Great. He's switched his sarcasm gun from *Stun* to *Kill*. I half turn in the seat, aim my gaze at him, fire off a warning round. But he's so irritated with me, and probably with Mason, and with this whole situation, that it seems he's temporarily immune.

I turn back.

"What are you trying to find?" I ask her, clicking in to her use of the word "mission."

She clears her throat.

"I'm trying to retrace my steps so I can keep something terrible from happening."

Detonation.

Explosion.

Blast wave.

"What's—" I shove my hands under my legs so she can't see how bad they're sweat-shaking. "What's the terrible thing?"

Mason looks up, studies Haze's mirrored, face-masked, knit-capped head for a moment in the rearview before saying, "Who are you guys supposed to be, anyway?"

"Who are *we* supposed to be?" he asks. "Who are *you* supposed to be?"

She locks her gaze on the road. "Interesting question. I guess when you put it that way, I'm *supposed* to be the daughter of a high-level militia leader." She checks her mirrors again. "What an unfortunate reality for both of us. You guys aren't NIM, are you?"

"NIM?"

"So what—are you Feds?"

"Why would you even ask us that?" Haze spews from the backseat. "We're sixteen, man."

"Well, it's hard to tell with all that shit you have on." I keep waiting for a smile to melt through the protective sheen on her face, but she's too tight, too guarded.

"So, what's your mission objective?" I ask. "Is it something about the militia?"

"Do you know where we are?" she asks.

"Not a clue," Haze pipes in, flat and dry, from the backseat. I'm not even looking at him anymore.

"Does the New Occidental fault line mean anything to you?"

"As in, seismic fault line?" I ask.

"As in, there's going to be a major event along this fault. As in, their experts have even given a window of time for the event to transpire. As in, these alleged experts have prophesized some kind of massive battle that's signaled by the ripping apart of the entire country right down this very line, sometime in the next forty-eight hours."

My head fills with the kind of frantic static you get between radio stations. *They brought this girl to us.* The commandos have led us right where we need to be: to the UpRising. But why Mason? Do I know her? Have we raided together before? It sounds like she's on a totally different mission than I am, and yet there's a massive clang of déjà vu with it too.

A rhythmic buzz hits my back pocket. I scramble to open it. Cockroach.

My gaze shoots out the window. I need to stay vigilant. Turk is turning up the heat, and suddenly my own theory, that the Battle of UpRising could start at any time, seems more plausible than ever. So much spark and sulfur in the air, I'd swear Turk's army is just around the corner.

"They're amassing swarms of militia members in towns all along the New Occidental," Mason continues. "And they're spreading their insane propaganda in hopes of inciting riots and panic."

Haze sits up, straightens himself out. This shit's right up his alley.

"Who's in charge?" he asks.

"A. B. Barshaw." She throws a nervous look against the review mirror. "My father."

Haze and I catch each other's eye.

"So . . . in the next forty-eight hours," Haze says, "there's supposed to be a major event somewhere along this New Occidental fault line?"

"That's right."

"Where *is* the fault line, exactly?" I ask.

She thrusts her chin toward the window. "We're driving alongside it."

My pulse clocks autobahn speeds. I fire up my Snipe page, start searching like a crazy person.

"What's the militia got to do with it?" Haze asks. "Earthquakes are an act of God."

Act of God . . . I switch back over to my messages, check to see if the commandos have snuck one through yet. To my huge relief, the envelope icon is blipping.

Fear will shake the world to its foundation.

"Uh, Haze," I say, hoping that Mason can't hear the worry in my voice.

I show him the new message. At first he just stares at the phone for a long time, but then he turns to look at Mason and then me in the same slow, deliberate way he changes TV stations.

Mason cranes over. "What is it?" she asks.

"I—it's—our friend broke an all-time scoring record in this video game we play. It's stupid."

She nods solemnly, eyes fixed on the road ahead.

Haze doesn't take his eyes off me. "You were saying?" he asks Mason.

"My father's group, the New Infantry Militia—NIM . . . they're deconstructionists. Conspiracy theorists. End-timers. They're the guys with subterranean bunkers and years' worth of food, fuel, and ammunition. They're ready and waiting for battle."

Subterranean bunkers? End-timers? Ready for battle?

The UnderGround. *The end is near.* Just like I thought. So why isn't she battling for UpRising?

In the minuscule beat of time that follows, I freeze-frame on Goofy Golf. On the old man videotaping my birthday party with a cigarette dangling from his mouth, on my mom looking shrink-wrapped in the corner, on the posse of sugar-buzzed boys wreaking havoc around the park.

Gone. All of it. In a flash. I shut my eyes against the blast wave of memory, feel the heat of it *sizzle-hiss* against my skin.

The end is near.

Only what if . . . ?

What if . . . ?

"So what are they after?" Haze asks her, the sound waves of his voice distorting the air around us.

"NIM has a plan in the works to reclaim sovereignty of the country. And I'm trying to figure out how to stop it. All I know is, they're prepared to fight to the very end to see this thing through. To the death."

Her words come through in slow motion, hit my head from a thousand different angles. I need a Medic. Someone's gonna need to throw me some massive heals, because I'm fading, man. I'm fading, and Haze is fading, and Mason's fading, and even when I close my eyes, all I can see is the same chilling phrase wavering above our heads where we should be solid green.

The end is near.

"Yeah, but they can't just make an earthquake happen," Haze says. "Can they?"

"You'd be shocked at what NIM can do." Mason scans the mirrors again. "They've already launched a string of so-called natural disasters."

"Like what?"

"A few minor earthquakes—practice drills, you could say. Forest fires. Wildlife die-offs."

I'm drop-kicked back into the conversation. "Wait, *wildlife die-offs?*"

"Yeah. You know. Birds. Fish. That sort of thing."

Birds . . .

I reach in my pocket, touch the feather I'd stashed there, wonder with a thousand-watt jolt of alarm if by having it, I'm somehow harboring the enemy.

"And the earthquake that's supposed to happen?" Haze presses.

The voice of the carny echo-twangs in my head.

Thunder and earthquake and great noise, with windstorm and tempest and flames of a devouring fire.

Mason swerves around a fallen tree branch in the road. I scan the horizon. Not a tree in sight.

She doesn't seem fazed.

"NIM's ultimate goal," she says, "is to implement a new order. It's all totally underground for now, which is why I need more info. But my guess is, once people hear about these quote-unquote natural disasters, they'll become terrified, seek help from a leadership that's strained and ineffective, at which point the movement sweeps in and—*bam*. It's the end of the world as we know it."

I formulate my next question about three dozen different ways in my head before I finally blurt out, "So who are you working with?"

She goes white, then pink at the question.

"No one."

Only something about her tone makes me veer toward not believing her.

"Is that why you're out here all alone?" I ask.

This time she throws me a look of borderline hostility.

"I'm alone because my father has no problem leaving his daughter to fend for herself while he goes off on some ridiculous salvage mission," she says. The words ricochet through the cab of the Jeep like small explosions. "I guess that's just what happens when a father's idea of salvation isn't the same as his daughter's. It's easy to think you're saving a world that doesn't bear any resemblance to the world you left behind."

I panic-dig in my bag for my earbuds, desperate for some Bunny Puke or Motor City, anything to drown out the mega-whir of chaos inside my head.

Bunny Puke proves effective. Until I spot the bright yellow dot barreling down the road toward us.

The three of us watch as it gets closer and closer, and suddenly my head glass shatters in a shred-of-metal, squeal-of-tires collision of denial versus reality.

The bug truck zips past us going double the speed limit in the other direction.

"Whoa," Haze says. "Was that Termi-Pest?"

"I don't know," I say.

The tang of panic rises in my throat.

Is it Stan? Is she with him?

I stare into the side-view mirror long after the yellow dot disappears.

"What are the odds of a Termi-Pest truck being all the way out here?" Haze says.

I lean backward over the seat. "Turn around," I tell Mason.

She takes her eyes off the road long enough to look at me like I'm crazy. *"What?"*

"Turn around! We need to follow that truck!"

"The hell," she says. "I'm on a mission—you guys are just along for the ride. If you want to follow that truck, you can get out and—"

"Holy shit, Tosh," Haze says, leaning forward to smack me on the shoulder. "Look!"

A second bug-mobile zips by less than a mile behind the first one. We're still watching it disappear in the rearview mirror when along comes another.

And another.

"Dude," Haze says. "This is biblical."

I check the phone, but there's nothing about a plague of cockroach trucks from the commandos or anyone else.

The next message does come through, though. Loud and clear.

Fear will shake the world to its foundation.

Just as I'm reading the message, it starts.

The ground beneath us lurches, and the road begins to buckle and roll, and all Mason has time to do is slam on the brakes before the entire road rips completely in two, right down the dotted yellow line.

- 19 -

The shaking goes on forever.

Seems like it, anyway. But eventually the tremor stops, and once it does, once the dust and debris settle, reality takes its grim shape in a panoramic arc around us.

The earth has unzipped.

The highway has split completely in two, and now the right side of the road is a half story down from the left side.

We are stalled out on the lower deck.

"Everyone okay?" Mason asks.

"Fine," Haze says from the back.

"*Mghunh*," I groan.

We manage to scramble out of the Jeep and stagger into the middle of the highway. Or what has become the middle of the highway, seeing as how the old middle is now an escalator ride up. The newly formed fissure surfs an asphalt wave as far as the eye can see in either direction as the three of us stand and survey the damage: puffs of black smoke off in the distance, pockets of flames burning through freshly ripped holes in the earth, toppled utility poles.

"It can't be," she whispers.

"What?" I ask.

"This can't be happening." Her voice sounds unimaginably soft compared to the hard, angry edges that have cracked open all around us. Quiet tears slide down her face as she takes it all in. "This can't be real. I thought it was just him, ranting like he always does. I thought if I followed him, caught him in his lies, I could . . . I just never thought anything like this would ever really happen."

The sadness in her eyes freeze-hardens, then cracks, as she zeros in on me close and tight. I was right about her. Mason Barshaw is no Supergirl. She's not like Elan, or Ravyn, or Starla Manley. Those girls weren't in trouble, and they didn't need to be rescued. But Mason Barshaw? I know just by looking, by listening, that Mason and I are both hostages to the same captor.

She wraps her fingers around my arm, tugs at me. "Now that it's starting, we'll be surrounded by NIM before we know it. And because of who I am, because of what I've done—" Her words break off, but the fear graffiti-paints itself across her face.

"They'll kill us," Haze says.

I turn away, spit onto the asphalt. I need to get my thoughts together, need to stay clearheaded. *I can map this one,* I tell myself. She doesn't need the extra worry.

But I can't pretend I'm not worried. I'm scared as all hell, in fact. I look over at Haze for guidance. Instead, he says:

"You just *had* to take that bug truck, didn't you?"

"Aw, Jesus, man, would you get off the bug truck for one second?"

"I told you not to do it, Tosh."

"You tell me not to do a lot of shit, Haze. If I listened to every single thing—"

"You guys!" Mason lifts her hand, points into the distance. "It doesn't matter. They're coming."

I look up, expecting to see a couple of Jeeps, maybe a four-wheel-drive pickup truck or two, and there are some of those, yes. But there's also a fleet of Humvees coming up from the south, and not the yuppie kind, either, but the military kind. As I squint to get a better look, I see . . . Yes, it is. It's a tank with a turret perched on top, and it's aimed in our direction.

"Do you think they'd really fire on us?" I ask.

"Let's not stick around to find out."

We clamber back into the Jeep, and I go limp with relief when the engine starts right up. Mason spins a wide brodie onto the shoulder before heading back up the highway the direction we came, sending us the wrong way on what is now a one-way road.

I wish *we* had a tank. Nothing wrong with a Jeep, but a tank would roll right over the top of anything in our way and absorb the hit from ammunition rounds a hell of a lot better than these plastic-wrap windows.

"Can you go any faster?" I ask.

"I'm doing ninety," she says. "How much faster do you want me to go?"

"A hundred would be good."

Mason drops her foot, and my body presses against the seat back from the jump in speed.

It's unearthly silent in the car.

Somewhere down the highway, once the seismic fissure veers into the grass and heads west, I notice a turnoff with just enough time to catch a fleeting glimpse of a road sign before Mason takes the ramp and follows the curve in a sharp arc. I grip the roll bar as we exit the highway going way faster than we should, and just like that, we're on a totally different highway, headed in a completely new direction.

She suddenly perks up. "Hey. You said your phone has GPS?"

"Yeah. Why?"

"There's this place out West that's supposed to be mega-spiritual."

A heavy thud hits the inside of my chest. *Somewhere spiritual.* It's on the list. My mom's list.

"Why do you want to go there?" I ask, fighting not to stumble over the words.

She glances into the rearview mirror, watching for signs of NIM, I'm sure.

"They say it's a healing place. Miracles, restoration, the whole chimichanga." She gives her lips a nervous lick. "If we make it that far," she adds.

A healing place.

I should have brought Devin.

I should have let him in my go-kart, should have brought him with me on this mission. Instead the old man carted him off somewhere, only he doesn't want to take care of him the right way, and now they're gone and I don't know where they are and don't even know if I can throw my brother a heal if he's not actually here.

The known will cease to exist.

Jesus, how does anyone keep going, knowing that might be true?

Mason points to the phone. "Fire it up."

I look at the screen, at the little red light flash-spasming up at me.

"I'm dying," I tell her.

"Oh. Use mine, then. It's in the glove box."

I shoot her a look.

"I have to hide it while I'm driving," she says. "I used to have a little problem."

Haze snorts in disgust but stops short at revealing that I made that mistake too.

A minuscule smile crosses Mason's face as I take her phone out and fire up the GPS. I try to smile back, want desperately to feel its reluctant pull at the corner of my mouth. But I can't.

"What am I looking for?" I ask instead.

Her eyes leave the road, start scanning the air. "I can't remember what it's called. How about typing in . . . ?" She darts a quick look at her phone and then at me. "'Spiritual West.'"

A dull throb starts in the epicenter of my chest cavity, radiates out in waves of invisible pain. I have no idea where Stan promised to take my mom. All I know is, she wanted to go somewhere spiritual.

I choke a little on the thought.

My phone buzzes from where I stashed it under my leg, and I open it, even though I probably shouldn't use up any unnecessary juice.

Fear will rock the world to its foundation.

Oh shit.

"Pull over," I tell her.

"What?"

"Pull over!"

She does, and within seconds, we're hit by a strong aftershock. The ground completely liquefies around us.

Mason spins on me as soon as the shaking stops.

"How'd you know that?" She searches my face like she's trying to read a map, and something in her eyes makes me want to do more than answer her. I want to tell her the truth.

I'm just not sure what the truth is anymore.

"We *are* in an area of heavy seismic activity," Haze says, pulling the answer out of his ass á la Roundhouse. "There's always more shaking after a quake."

I'm impressed. Not that I'd tell *him* that; I haven't forgotten we're still in the middle of a fight.

She shakes her head in awe as we get back on the road and continue southwest, stopping every few miles to let the ground buckle beneath us. Between the aftershocks and the NIM convoy, which I'm sure must have us on its radar again by now, I keep checking out the windows, waiting for the other combat boot to drop.

From time to time, I sneak-look at Mason, watch the Supergirl logo on her shirt rise and fall with each frightened breath. My phone continues to buzz the same way it has right before each aftershock, and each time, I warn her to pull over. She has no idea I'm getting advanced insider information about the quakes, but she looks at me like I'm Einstein every time it happens, so I only feel a little bad.

"God," she says as we pull back onto the highway. "You're like a human Richter scale."

"Now you know my superpower," I say. "You have to swear your undying secrecy and allegiance forever."

I've finally managed to get a full-blown smile out of her. Dimples crease the space between her cheeks and her chin, and faint lines feather out the sides of her eyes. The bigger she smiles, the more her mouth pulls slightly to one side, and I decide then and there that it could easily be my new mission just to make that happen again.

"It's a deal," she says.

We hang out in that unblinking moment: me, tethered to Mason by a lame joke that had the power to make her smile, and her, distracted from driving by a gaming geek from Sandusky, Ohio. Just then, Haze shouts, "Watch out!" and Mason slams on the brakes. But it's not enough to keep us from careening into a massive pile of twisted yellow metal.

For a terrifying moment, the world is a blur of jagged edges and crushed glass and torn canvas and smoke and blood and asphalt, but eventually it stops and we come to a rest, upright and mostly unscathed. We take a few seconds to catch our breath, and then . . .

It can't be.

It's not possible.

But it's true.

We're knotted up in a mangled dog pile of Termi-Pest trucks.

– 19.5 –

Mason says she's stuck, so I whip around to her side of the Jeep for an assist. Haze falls out after her.

We cough into the smoke-filled air, wave it away from our faces. I watch as she takes a bandanna out of her pocket, as she ties it around her nose and mouth to help her breathe.

My mouth slowly falls open.

I know her.

Mason Barshaw.

I absolutely know who she is.

- 20 -

"**Look at that,**" she whispers.

I peel my eyes away from her, cast a glance over my shoulder, spin the rest of the way around.

It's the most chilling thing I've ever seen.

Larger-than-life cockroaches, a dozen or so of them, lie scattered all over the highway, like mutant insects in one of those black-and-white Japanese horror movies.

Even worse, the Jeep is totaled.

We pull our stowed bags from behind the seats and start picking through the massive wreckage, but a low murmur pulls my attention to an area off the side of the road, about fifty yards past the hissing pile of bug-mobile carnage. I crane my neck until I see that the Termi-Pest drivers have congregated together like a Dickies-clad battalion, talking in hushed tones that carry easily across the flat landscape, and suddenly I know down to the microscopic fibers of my being that one of those guys is Stan.

To hell with Turk's lair. I've got Turk right here in my sights, right in the middle of his fucking army.

I lunge forward, and almost on cue, the men spot me. They stir, agitated, like a nest of hornets that's been disturbed.

They spread out, take a defensive posture.

"Stan?" I call out. "*Stan!* Show your face, you coward!" I start jogging toward them. "I know you're here, you sonofabitch! Where is she? *Where is she?*"

Mason calls after me.

So does Haze.

"Tosh!"

But all I want to do right now is go pummel the shit out of Stan, so I block Haze out. And Mason too. Only that's a lot harder because she sounds scared and worried. I'm already mad at Haze, but I don't know what to do with scared and worried. Never did. Never knew what to say to my mom when she got that way.

By the time I reach the bug guys, they're shoulder-to-shoulder in solidarity.

"*Stan!*"

I scan the faces, searching for a blip of familiarity while the echo of work boots landing flat on wooden steps ripples in the air, and the shouts of anger and accusation, of Cam screaming in one ear to get in the fight and Haze in the other telling me to get out of it, and the shatter of a maroon lamp across the brick walkway, and the blood.

The blood.

"*Stan!*" I scream, because I'm ready for this fight. Because I've been ready for this fight for a long time. But it doesn't matter now.

Stan isn't here.

And neither is my mom.

Only now I'm trapped toe-to-toe with an army of bug guys in gray Dickies, ready to exterminate at will if it should come to that.

I push my hands into my eye sockets and drop to my knees in the middle of the highway, stunned yet again by what an oxygen-sucking failure I am.

I finally got the chance to take the guy down, to tell him what I really think of him and his putrid pest-control truck and his carefully concealed ass crack and his utter ineptitude at extermination because he and my mom hadn't been gone for five fucking minutes before our place was crawling with cockroaches again and everything went to hell and the known ceased to exist.

I finally had the chance to become Worthy.

And I wiped.

− 20.5 −

Mason tries to comfort me with soft words and kindness, but I won't let her. She doesn't know me—what a failure I am, what a worthless son, brother, friend.

I can't even finish this one single mission without wiping.

Don't follow me, I tell them inside my head. *I don't deserve a buff.*

I shrug them off and head down the road alone.

- 21 -

I don't make it very far.

Haze and Mason come trotting up, fall in alongside me, flank me like a couple of dps.

But I don't want them here. I don't even want to be here. I just wish I could discard my body on the side of the road like a dirty T-shirt and let whatever blip of energy is left inside me just dissolve into the cosmos.

I look around as we walk, try to absorb the magnitude of destruction from an earthquake that was powerful enough to wreak havoc across this kind of distance.

The sound of gravel and glass crunching underfoot fills the space around us. Bits and pieces of things that used to be whole, reduced to fragments insignificant enough for the three of us to walk on top of without giving it the slightest thought.

"That was weird back there," Mason finally says. "With the bug trucks."

Haze comes in, right on cue. "I know, right? We have bug trucks just like that back home."

"No kidding?"

"Yeah. In fact, Tosh and I—"

But a low rumbling in the distance shuts him up before I can stop him from finishing the thought myself. The three of us spin in our tracks, disoriented as we watch and wait. I shade my eyes against the brightest part of the sky, but the rumbling just gets louder, cuts through the air like a machete-wielding psychopath. My heart drops into my feet, my feet bolt themselves to the road, and the road buckles and jolts beneath us as the military convoy we thought we'd fled back on that other map rolls into view in the distance.

"Shit," Haze whispers.

By now we've walked far enough down the road that there's nothing left to hide behind. We're down to one option.

Crouch.

I've seen the crouch maneuver before, usually in movies or on TV—it always looks like an exercise in futility. But I challenge you to walk down a deserted highway in the middle of the Boneyard and have a convoy of paramilitary militia descend on you that would just as soon see you dead as breathing, and *not* crouch in the middle of the road.

It doesn't end with the convoy, though.

The rumbling gets louder, more dissonant, and before we can sort out one sound from another, a swarm of Chinook helicopters sweeps the horizon, heading straight for us like a flock of militant blackbirds.

There are too many to count.

A vein of jagged, steely terror rips the length of my spine.

"The UpRising," I say, at the same moment Mason says, "It's the Showdown."

Haze swings on her. "The Showdown?"

"I'm not even on that expedition," I tell her.

"Yes, you are," she says in a whisper. "You've been on it the whole time."

I want to argue the point. I should know what battle I've been fighting, right? I mean, it's *my* battle. But when she turns to me, her hair kicking up around her face under a Chinook-generated wind, all I can think about is how her eyes remind me of pictures of Earth taken from outer space: same shade of blue, filled with clouds and water.

"I can't believe this is happening," she says. "I did this. I never figured out how to stop it from coming."

The words echo-stutter inside my head. I've lost count of how many times I've told myself the same thing.

I watch as Mason uses her fingertips to wipe tears from under her eyes, and I ache to reach out, wipe the tears away for her so she doesn't have to touch her own sadness. But I can't. I can't move, can't speak, can't help her, can't comfort her, can't think, can't act, just like the day my mom left—I just stood there and watched the truck drive away and did nothing.

Mason shudders.

"Let's get the hell out of here," Haze says. "They'll probably open fire any second."

But I don't budge. Instead I frantically dig around inside my coat pocket until I find the blackbird feather, run it between my fingers, wonder why it ended up on my Trade Screen in the first place. The only purpose that feather serves is a reminder. A terrible reminder of that one moment in time.

When the known ceased to exist.

"C'mon, Tosh!" Haze shouts as a swarm of Chinooks fills the sky overhead.

A message vibrates right through my back pocket. I can't even be sure it's Turk anymore, since I don't seem to be raiding for UpRising now. I take it out, open the app to check.

"Tosh!"

"I'm coming!"

The worthy shall sacrifice the lamb.

A rapid-fire series of snapshots follows. Devin. The cockroach. A dead bird.

Holy shit.

Haze is right; we have to get out of here, fast.

But where? How?

By now we're flanked on one side by a brigade of militia vehicles and on the other by a squadron of hovering Chinooks.

We're trapped.

I tap Haze on the arm to get his attention since it's too loud to even hear my own thoughts, show him the new message, hope he knows what it means. But all he does is wave for us to follow him. We start jogging down the highway. I'm sure we look ridiculous, trying to outrun both a massive paramilitary convoy and a fleet of dual-propeller helicopters.

The worthy shall sacrifice the lamb.

I'm dripping with terror and sweat.

The Chinooks have stopped flying and are now hovering above us, blanketing the entire area between us and the convoy. That is, until the lead chopper breaks away, threads a route back through the others, and begins to track us.

My panic meter shoots off the charts.

We bust into a sprint, ducking and weaving, even though I know damn well there's no way to outrun a helicopter. But I also know we have to try, because the alternative to trying is giving up, and I can't do that. I've failed so many times, lost so many breaks. . . . This could be the last chance I ever have to get this right.

The Chinook stays on our tail. It doesn't corral us or block us by landing on the road; it just trails us for what seems like an eternity. In the distance, I can hear the exchange of rifle and mortar fire between the Humvees and tanks on the ground and the helicopters hovering above them. At least we managed to avoid that melee.

I feel like we just ran ten miles, but I bet it's only a fraction of that. Still, it seems like I should be more winded than I am, more fatigued, on the verge of collapse. But I'm not. I'm full green and still running—probably on pure adrenaline.

It isn't until we're out of earshot of the gunfire that the helicopter begins dropping. It sinks lower and lower until it's close enough to grab, and I'm seriously tripping out, darting all over the road while the three of us braid a line of confusion in one final, futile attempt to throw them off.

As the chopper lands in front of us, we try crouching again.

That's when a trio of soldiers clad in black, gray, and purple camouflage piles out of the Chinook, sweeping their weps in a panoramic arc around us, their bowl-cut hairdos flapping in the wind.

My relief at seeing the commandos is so far off the charts, I swear I want to run up and hug them. But my elation is short-lived. There's no glint of recognition on their part, no welcome committee, no "Thank you for getting things this far, Tosh," no "We knew we could count on you." No "You are Worthy."

"Mason Emily Barshaw," one of the soldiers calls out. "You are ordered to board this aircraft."

"On whose authority?" Haze barks back.

The soldier goes max-red stance, and I glance over my shoulder, sure he's about to draw aggro and we'll all get caught in the crossfire. "On the authority of—"

"That is classified information!" his comrade cuts in.

"On what grounds, then?"

"That is classified."

I flick a nanoglance at Mason, who looks pound for pound as confused as I am.

I'm heading into a full-body sweat-shake.

"Who sent you?" she shouts over the noise, but the commando just waves us toward the chopper. "Let's go! We can only hold 'em off for so long."

Against my fear and better judgment, I push Mason toward the helicopter, where the other two commandos help us climb aboard. We lift off the second the last commando's foot leaves the ground, speeding in the opposite direction of the raid raging a few miles behind us.

Mason swings toward the rifle-wielding soldier. "How did you know where to find me?" she asks. "How do you even know who I am?"

She has to shout over the noise inside the Chinook. Something about the rhythmic rotation of the propeller blades shakes me down to my bones.

"Your signatures," he shouts back. His buddy flashes him a look of warning.

But Mason doesn't understand the answer, and I'm not sure I do either.

"Where are you taking us?" Haze asks.

"That is classified information."

I don't get it. I thought these guys had been tracking me this whole time, watching my progress. Prepping me for battle. I thought they were loading my Trade Screen with rations and weps, all the things I'd need to Ascend. Only, here they are on Mason's expedition. They don't even seem to recognize me. Jesus, it's like looking at Devin—complete blank screen. I don't know what to think anymore, except that maybe I got massive hacked.

Mason leans over, puts her face right up to the side of my head, whispers so the commandos can't hear, "No worries. We're both going the same way. I promise."

I arc in a semicircle toward her, lock eyes with her for a long, questioning moment. Her face mimics the hills and valleys of the landscape below us, and I wish I could reach over, smooth out the lines of worry on her forehead, upturn the corners of her mouth, flatten the ridges of fear between her eyebrows. If I could just force my hand to make the short trip from my lap to her cheek . . .

I shift in my seat like I'm going to rest my arm on the metal bar behind us, but instead I let it brush against her hair. She looks at me without flinching, and I'm caught in that space between breathing and not, between knowing everything and knowing nothing. I hold my breath, move my fingertips lightly across her forehead, run my thumb over her folded brow, brush a strand of hair out of her eyelashes before I pull away again. She smiles, just barely, but enough to make those tiny dimples show up next to her chin.

"And yes," she whispers. "I know who you are."

I lean in to Mason Barshaw, Militiababe, as she turns to look out the window. No wonder she wants to go to the healing grounds of the spiritual West: she's a Medic. Her whole job is healing.

I shudder with the inexplicable relief of knowing I was finally right about something.

Except now I know that being right could prove deadly. I haven't been able to stop thinking about the last message I got, about how the worthy shall sacrifice the lamb. My ears start to fill with the bleating cries of lambs being led to the slaughter. One by one, taken unknowingly to some unseen place, only to disappear forever.

I hope to God that's not what the old man did with Devin.

I shudder, let my gaze drift through the inner cavity of the Chinook. Haze hasn't taken his eyes off the chopper pilot for one second, Mason's scouting the landscape below, probably looking for signs of the Showdown, and I have no idea how long this nine-hour UpRising expedition has actually gone on, only that it feels like forever.

That's the kicker about loss. It does strange things to time, stretching it out long and wide so it becomes this eternal, bloated entity.

I pull out my phone, check my home screen. The clock reads ten to four.

Ten to four? But that would mean—

The pilot calls out from up front, "Prepare to land!"

I peer out the window, notice a large rectangle of dirt with two metal-roofed hangars down at one end. The commandos make no announcement about where we are or what the land-mark is below us, but it sure as hell doesn't look like a helipad. In fact, if this is an airbase, it's the most illegitimate airbase ever.

As we fly over, I notice the rotors sound different. Not good different. Bad different. Grinding metal-on-metal different.

Haze notices it too.

"Is something wrong with the—"

"Stay seated. Be sure you're buckled in," the pilot barks. "Touchdown is going to be rough."

He cuts off the last word, because the chopper has started listing, kicking up a flurry of activity in the cockpit and a huge amount of dust below. For a second I worry about what happens if those clouds of dirt get caught in the rotor blades, and then I realize that we're in shit up to our elbows already—a little extra dirt isn't likely to change that fact.

Mason grabs on to my hand, and the three of us brace ourselves for impact.

"Rough" doesn't begin to cover it.

The chopper hits the ground with a deafening *thud*, dropping immediately onto its side, where the propeller blades spin themselves into oblivion against the dirt. Chunks of metal go flying everywhere; some even break through the fuselage of the Chinook, sending a spray of glass through the helicopter like a shaken soda bottle.

It takes forever for the pilot to cut the engines, so long, in fact, that I wonder if they're actually *trying* to kill us.

My internal alarms go Code Orange when I realize I'm not the slightest bit hurt.

As soon as the motors and rotors have groaned into silence, one of the commandos rushes up to Mason, unbuckles her, and throws her over his shoulder, carrying her out to safety. So much for me and Haze, apparently.

I look around the dust-choked interior of the helicopter, but I don't see anyone else inside.

"Haze?" I call out, wait for something to come back.

Outside the wreckage, I hear Mason shouting at the commando.

"Get off me! What the hell just happened?"

"This area is known to experience energy fluctuations," he says. Even from my seat, where I'm stuck struggling to free myself from these ridiculously complex military harnesses, I hear something in his voice that chills me. "Sometimes those fluctuations confuse the machinery."

I don't believe him for a second.

I have to free myself, see what's going on.

"Yo, Haze?" I call out again. He couldn't have gone too far; the guy was sitting right here two seconds ago.

By now I really wish I hadn't lost my goggles—I can barely see anything in all the smoke and dust. All I know is, Haze must have hopped out already. I'm not sure how.

I reach for my gear and . . .

Face mask.

Haze's face mask is attached to the strap of my bag.

Only Haze is still nowhere to be seen.

I panic-fight to untangle myself from the safety harness. The second I'm free, I clamber to get to the door of the sunny-side up helicopter.

"I demand to know where we are," Mason says, her tone low and firm, like she's used to being in charge.

"We did not make it all the way to the airbase."

"Where's my friend?" I yell, stumbling out of the Chinook.

Mason cocks her head at me like a confused puppy.

The commandos stand in mute attention. Before they were purposefully vague, but now they're blatantly refusing to answer me.

"Where's my friend?"

Mason puts her hand on my arm, but I shrug her off.

"Tosh—"

"No! My friend . . . Haze . . . was on the helicopter with us. *He was on the helicopter with us*, and now he's not!"

The commando fingers his rifle. "I'm going to have to ask you to calm down."

"Tosh," Mason says, trying to soothe me, trying to placate me, like she's in on it somehow, like *this* is the conspiracy.

I lunge at the commando, but she holds me back. It stops me cold for a second, how strong she is. I was not expecting that.

"Where. Is. My. Friend?" I'm panting, leeching sweat and spit everywhere.

The commando elbows me aside, leans in to Mason closer than she's clearly comfortable with.

"Ms. Barshaw," he says in a half whisper. "A few moments from now, a vehicle will come by to pick you up. They're going to take you to a safe house. We need to get you off the radar."

She gazes into the distance, her deep blue eyes filling with tears that she quickly blinks away. She nods without looking at him.

They're starting to break her down.

"I'm going to need your phone," he tells her, holding his hand out, palm up.

Wait a minute. She didn't do anything—why is she losing weps? What kind of platoon leader strips you of your battle gear for no legitimate reason?

"No!" I call out, body-blocking Mason. "You don't have the authority to—"

Mason's grip tightens so hard around my arm, it starts to tingle. She turns her head, speaks to me over her shoulder.

"If you don't stop talking crazy, you'll get left behind. We can't afford to lose each other."

She comes back a half turn, holds my gaze a few seconds before letting me go. Without taking her eyes off me, she fishes her cell phone out of her bag and hands it over.

The airman pries open the back, digs out the battery and the SIM card, pockets them, hands the phone back to her the way the commandos handed me that dead bird in Sandusky. She reluctantly takes it.

Seconds later, a VW van chugs up next to us. It's painted the same black-gray-purple motif as the commandos' fatigues, only the van sports tracks instead of tires, like an armored tank. The commando ushers her into the front seat. I stand there, checking and rechecking for Haze over my shoulder, until the commando impatiently waves me over and points to the back. I'm not even all the way in before the van takes off again.

I crush my bag against my chest, grip Haze's face mask with both hands, fight back a wave of tears.

"Sit tight," the driver hollers over all the racket. "Ride's gonna be bumpy!"

I twist around, watch the smoldering helicopter wreck disappear over my shoulder as we speed off, hoping to catch a glimpse of Haze so I can yell at the driver to stop, to go back, to save him.

How could I have let this happen? The first rule of combat is:

never leave a platoon member behind. Abandon no fellow soldier, ever.

I grip my chest against the memory.

Two truck doors.

One slamming right after the other.

And then she left.

- 21.5 -

Mason and I are on the same mission.

- 22 -

Before long, we roll up to the entrance of an adobe church. Mason barely waits for the driver to cut the engine before asking, "What is this place?"

"El Sanctuario." His overexaggerated pronunciation makes me cringe.

As we pile out of the van, I fully expect further instructions from the driver, or maybe even for a nun to come out and escort us inside.

But no.

"What do we do now?" Mason asks the driver.

"Go inside," he says. "And wait."

"Wait for what?" she calls after him as he grinds the gears and sputters off down the road.

We spend a few seconds looking at the smooth mocha-brown facade of the church, at the adobe fence with its rickety wooden gate standing in an open invitation to enter, which we do. Just inside the courtyard, a rugged wooden cross is meant to let visitors know they are in a spiritual place.

Somewhere spiritual.

That's what she wanted.

Learn to fly. Fly away. Somewhere spiritual.

The ache radiates from my organs and cells into the clay and dust and cactus of El Sanctuario.

Mason reaches for my hand, slides her fingers through mine, and I manage somehow to slip back into myself without rupturing.

She seems to have taken a vow of silence as we wander the grounds, through the crosses that occupy nearly every inch of vertical surface. Wrought iron, wood, bamboo—they hang on every fence, stand planted in adobe bases, some are even draped with rosary beads. I've never seen a map that was so littered with religious icons—this is most definitely not my version of the Boneyard.

Mason tugs my hand, and I follow her as she tiptoes into the chapel.

The only light inside comes from sun pouring in through the windows and from small burning candles along nearly every wall. Mason sits on one of the flat wooden pews but doesn't motion me to join her, so I just keep moving through the high-ceilinged sanctuary. For some reason, I need to touch everything, to get the feel of this place on my fingers. The wooden shelves that hold up rows of votives. The hand-painted pictures of saints and angels. Wrought-iron candelabras. A statue of the Virgin Mary, tucked into a small arch carved into the wall. Shadow and light fall over the Virgin's face, and I lean in, run my fingers along the curve of her royal-blue veil. Flashes of memory hit me quick and hard. Devin's Virgin Mary skateboard. The I-Tech raiders decked out in the same shade of blue.

I pull my hand back, look closer at the carved face, at the hair painted the same soft brown as my mom's. The eyes cast downward. The lips bent in eternal sadness, as if the woman in the statue always knew her heart would break someday.

I close my eyes, watch my mom getting into Stan's truck that late afternoon, the way she leaned out the window for one last look at me as I stood there choked with paralyzing grief. I open my eyes again, stroke the statue, think how strange it is that the shadows fall across its face in exactly the same way.

In a flash, it's hot inside the sanctuary—boiling hot, like in the subway catacombs. Sweat pools, then pours down my neck and back. I find an open doorway, slip outside for some cool air.

I end up in a courtyard somewhere in the center of the sanctuary. Get my bearings. Start walking. Follow the high adobe fence that surrounds the complex until I hit another, smaller courtyard. Here, a man-made rock structure houses some kind of built-in shrine with a tiled picture of the Virgin Mary resting against the back wall and a statuette of Jesus kneeling before her. Bouquets of fresh-cut flowers sit at her feet, and rows of rosary beads that I'm guessing people leave behind after saying a prayer hang from a rod across the top. The bottom is covered in candles, most of them lit.

I wonder how many of those rosary prayers were answered.

I wonder if that's why my mom wanted to visit a place like this.

I follow the fence around to the back of the sanctuary, where I stumble across a weedy, overgrown cemetery. The markers are homemade stone-and-iron tributes, and every single grave is decorated with flowers—freshly cut, brightly colored flowers.

It's strange, this place, confusing. The sanctuary is quiet and empty. The whitewashed walls remind me of the hotel where we met the Prophets, down to the dark outlines of accent wood throughout the chapel and the layers of dust coating the pews and pictures. But this place isn't like the hotel, or the school, or any of the rest of the maps on UpRising. It's not dead or abandoned; little signs of life exist everywhere I look. The lit candles. The fresh flowers. It's almost like I'm not in the Boneyard anymore, like I'm playing a completely different game. Even though it confuses me, I like it here. I like the calm, the safety of it. I haven't been anywhere this serene in at least1,580-some-odd days.

I find my way back inside, relieved that Mason's still sitting in the pew. She might be praying or might not—I can't tell. Doesn't matter. Either way my mission in this moment is to let her be, to do whatever it is she wants to do here. Maybe she *needed* to come to a place like this. I'm not sure why I think that, just that it's the first truth I've felt in a long time.

At the far end of the room I spot a table filled with mostly lit votives, and I wander over to it, wondering if it would be disrespectful to light a candle when I'm not even Catholic. They must have a sign posted, something that says what you're supposed to do. But all I see is a Bible lying open on the table. It's old, has that look like it's printed on onionskin, on paper so thin you could tear it just by looking too hard. I hold my breath, lean in just barely. I don't know much about the Bible, only that this one is open to Genesis, and that "genesis" means "beginning," and I think how strange that is, too, since I only seem to be steered toward endings. Bad ones. But I read what's on the page anyway.

It's the story of Abraham.

It's the story of how God wants Abraham to sacrifice his only son, Isaac.

God wants Abraham to sacrifice his son.

Devin.

The worthy will sacrifice the lamb.

Mason.

I freeze for a second, then sprint into the pews, only to find them empty.

The pew.

The chapel.

The whole fucking sanctuary.

Empty.

I spin around a few times. Maybe she went outside like I did, to get some fresh air. Maybe she went out to look for me. I stagger through the courtyard, along the fence, down by the cemetery, scan the entire space around me, every inch. Fear peels off me in sheets as I realize . . .

She's gone.

Mason.

Is.

Gone.

- 23 -

I don't even get two seconds to ponder the thought.

The entire building begins to rumble. I hit the deck, waiting for it to stop, but it doesn't, so I lay panting on the floor, breathing in dirt and dust and microscopic particles of things that used to be whole, and then I see them: cockroach after cockroach heading straight at me across the floor. I squeeze my eyes shut, wishing to hell I knew what I did wrong this time. Every time. Everyone. Gone.

I have to get out of here.

I scramble to my feet, run into the chapel, but the shaking and rumbling just get louder, stronger. A cloud of dust blows in through the open doors. It takes a while for enough of it to clear away to reveal the outline of soldiers storming the sanctuary courtyard. I can't tell if they're commandos or NIM—the dust is still too thick to make out any details.

As they burst into the chapel, my eyes go straight to their gray-purple-black fatigues. I don't know why, but their presence is not completely reassuring this time.

"What is this?" I call out. "Why are you back?"

"The area is compromised."

No shit. "Where's Mason?"

The commandos spread out, search the chapel and the courtyard, leaving two men in the room with me, weps at the ready.

"*Where is she?*" I yell.

The others return to the chapel, shake their bowl-cut heads in silent affirmation.

I'm the only one here.

"She can't be gone. . . ." My words ricochet against the vaulted ceiling, then hurl back down to the dirt floor. "I saved her. Jesus, man, I got her here. How can she be gone?"

"Your signatures," says the commando with the barrel leveled at my chest.

"*My* signatures?"

"Your movements," he says, impatient.

The blood drains completely out of my body, spills into a crimson pool around my feet.

I did this?

My phone. My signals. My signature.

My fault.

"She's gone?" I ask. No amount of blinking can outmaneuver the flow of tears hitting my eyes.

The commandos say nothing.

"Was it NIM?" I demand.

Silence.

"Where'd they take her?"

Silence.

"Why did you ask for my help after the bird die-off?"

Silence.

The absoluteness of nothing.

"I was supposed to help," I say, fighting to keep the break out of my voice. "I was supposed to save it. I thought you wanted me to save it."

"It was your signatures," he says again.

They swarm in as my knees give out, grab me as I start to fall. As the room freeze-frames around me, they prevent me from total collapse onto the floor.

"*I* did this." The words rip out of me, grinding, shrieking, metal on metal. "I made it happen. I couldn't fix it."

"It was your signatures."

I try to pull away. "*I know.* You fucking told me that already!" I free one arm from the commando's grip, reach into my pocket, pull out my phone.

I shove it at him.

The commando hesitates for a half beat, then grabs the phone and disembowels it before handing the empty shell to his fellow soldier.

"Now cuff him," he says.

What?

"Cuff me? Why?"

The commando jerks my hands behind my back, wraps zip ties around my wrists, and pulls tight.

"Why are you doing this? Aren't we on the same side?"

"You can't help us," he says. "And we can't help you."

No one can help you, Ravyn had said.

And just as they begin to drag me toward the awaiting Jeep, I catch the first glimpse of the patch on his arm, the almost minuscule embroidered letters:

NIM.

- 23.5 -

I ran after her at first, in complete shock.

In disbelief.

She was leaving. And I couldn't speak.

Couldn't scream.

Couldn't stop her.

And then I just stood there, crap-excuse-of-a-loser-son that I am, and watched her go.

- 24 -

All I can do is kick and rant as they lift me by the arms and legs and carry me toward a waiting Jeep.

"Shut up," one of the commandos snaps.

"Make me."

He accepts the challenge.

My heavy head throbs like a bitch, but I keep shouting for Haze and Mason even after the commando's thrown me into the back of his covered truck. If he wants me to shut up, he'll have to muzzle me. Or shoot me.

I hear the engine start up and the gears grind, and I topple backward as the truck lurches forward.

I scream, but they don't answer me. I bang my head against the thick plastic window, kick at the sides, slam my feet against the truck liner, knowing they could stop at any minute, come back here, beat the crap out of me, or worse.

But they don't pull over, don't stop. They don't even turn

around in their seats. It's like they can't hear me. Like I don't exist.

You mustn't question the mission.

Son of a bitch. Oldest trick in the book and I fell for it like an idiot supreme. Played right into their hands. Delivered the last two people in the world I could trust right to them on a silver fucking platter, the whole time thinking I could still be Worthy, that I could Ascend.

No one can save you.

I can't accept that as reality. I can't.

I lean against the truck wall, watch somewhere spiritual shrink into the distance.

My eyelids close. I feel the drift of the truck moving through time and space, and I wonder if this is what it feels like to die. Weightless, painless, floating on the jet stream of the universe. I'd do anything to stop the ache, the constant gaping, bleeding, infected wound that never heals, never closes over, just sits there, raw and oozing, every minute of every day.

I know I should stay awake, that it would be a tactical mistake to drift off. But I'm so tired, I'm not sure I can fight it.

I'm tired of having to fight.

My head kicks straight up off the corrugated metal truck bed as we hit a pothole or something. I'm not even fully awake yet before I come down again, hard enough to get serious cranial reverb.

Massive headache now added to the groggy, but it still isn't enough to pull me out of this deep, narcoleptic-grade sleep I'm in. I drift off again.

I have no idea how long I've been in the back of this truck, only that at some point my eyelids fly open as I realize we're not moving anymore. I lean up, get my bearings, notice that I'm covered in a wool army blanket, as if someone tucked me in somewhere along the way.

I worm my way to my knees, crawl to the back window, push my head through the plastic flap. We're definitely stopped, but I have no idea where. It looks pretty woodsy, and the air smells like a Christmas tree in February, like a pine air freshener that's almost but not quite used up. Patches of bright blue sky hang between huge thunderheads over the tree line, only for some reason I can see the Carew Tower sticking up between the tips of two soaring redwoods, and it's tripping my shit because I feel like I'm as far from home as I've ever been.

"Hello?" I call out, my voice echoing flat and hollow back to me. "Anyone there?"

No answer.

I immediately start calculating how I can climb out of the back of this truck without needing to use my hands. I'd like to keep from falling out if possible, because (a) that would look ridiculous if anyone's watching, and (b) if no one *is* watching, I'd probably end up cracking my head open on the asphalt and bleeding to death in the process, and I just lost the only person who could throw me a rez or even a heal.

I try standing, but the canopy is too low for me to get any higher than a hunch. That doesn't stop me from attempting to swing one leg over the back anyway. But the bumper is also too low and I avert castration-by-tailgate by a few minuscule centimeters.

I drop back inside, not ready to give up yet. There has to be a way out of this.

My Trade Screen is completely blank by now, thanks to my endless string of failures. I scout the bed of the truck for anything sharp enough or at least sturdy enough to saw through a hard plastic zip tie. Other than the military-issue blankets, there isn't so much as a used Spork back here.

Plan B: work my hands out of the cuff by bending and flexing, Houdini-style, until they slip through.

Plan B may take a while, though, partly because it's not as easy as they make it look on TV, and partly because my arms have fallen asleep—arms that don't have a whole lot of muscle tone in them in the first place.

As I wriggle my fingers and wrists in various states of contortion, I keep my ears open for the sounds of voices or footsteps or even tires coming down the road. Amazing what you can be attuned to without an earful of Bunny Puke slamming into your head.

My hands are nerve-sweating so bad by now, the zip tie actually starts to give a little. I get it up around my left wrist, nearly fold my hand in half to yank it all the way out. My arm muscles burn like crazy, but then . . .

Freedom.

Or so I think.

I tip my head, cue in to the crunch of footsteps on gravel echoing somewhere nearby. They're faint, but they're there, and I close my eyes against the translucent memory of Stan, his boots, our walkway. I shake the memory out of my head, lift the back window flap, catch a quick look around. Wherever those footsteps are coming from, it isn't behind the truck. I slip over the tailgate, proud as hell at how stealth I'm managing my escape as a prisoner of war.

But I'm not out of the weeds yet.

Can't let myself get lost in the details.

I peek around the side of the truck: the driver's side is clear too. I crouch as low as I can get and tiptoe around to the door. No time to wuss out. I press the button, ease the door open, crap myself with relief that no one's inside, and close the door as soft as possible after climbing in. A quick glance out the front window reveals nothing but wilderness. Which means those footsteps didn't come from in front of me either.

I bend down, check near the steering column, where, sure enough, the keys are in the ignition. I shake my head, stunned by this turn of good fortune. Maybe this is a reward drop from the expansion pack. Hell, I deserve *something* for staying in the game this long against all odds.

I'm fully aware that if there's a platoon within the slightest radius of this truck, it'll be instantaneously obvious, because as soon as I fire up the engine, they'll all come running. But the only alternative is to not start the engine, and if I stay here—

If you get in that car and drive away, you really are crazy.

If I stay here, I'm even crazier.

Echoes of Haze's voice ricochet off the tree bark, crash into echoes of mine, fuse together like twisted metal, careen into my head through my ear holes and tear ducts and up my nose into my brain matter, burrowing into my amygdala, sending me deep into fight-or-flight mode.

I'm not crazy.

I just want to save it.

I want to keep the end from coming, man.

All I need is one chance to make things right again.

- 25 -

As soon as the engine is running, the woods around me spring to life and I'm surrounded by every manner of weps, drawn and aimed straight at me.

I quick lock the doors before pushing against the clutch as hard as I can—not an easy task with my foot shaking uncontrollably. But I jam the gears anyway, cringing as they grunt and grind until I find the right one, and not a second too soon.

I gun it, and the soldiers roach-scatter away from the vehicle.

Once I'm in the clear, I start machete-wielding through my own head, try not to panic, get my thoughts sorted out, watch for landmarks so I can at least figure out where the hell I am since I don't have a mapper. At this rate, I'll never bank enough Ascent Credits to become Worthy.

I don't even know who I'm raiding for anymore.

Don't get me wrong. It's not that I mind raiding for Showdown. Something about Mason's mission felt so real to me, so familiar. I *wanted* to help her. I still do. But before I can be of any use to her, I need to finish my own battle.

The *tick-tick-ticking* of the mantel clock is so earsplitting loud, I can barely hear my own thoughts. Not to mention, it takes an impossible level of exertion to stay in the seat during the rugged trip down the mountain passage.

I'm doggedly fighting the ride when out of nowhere comes an entire battalion of soldiers looking hell-bent to stop me.

Or kill me.

This is dire. I have no weps, no platoon, no dps. I don't even have a phone. All I can do is dodge the AoE spread that comes at me and drop the pedal to the floor. The trees are closing in on me tight and the road begins to narrow. But I don't want to slow down, not even to take the curves. I can't afford to get caught in the crossfire.

But the next turn is a full three-sixty hairpin so sharp I have no choice but to pull my speed back to near nothing. When I finally push through it, the trees thin out just a little and the road widens up a bit, and that's when it starts raining birds.

Blackbirds.

By the hundreds.

I swerve to miss them, until I realize how dangerously stupid it is to swerve on a winding mountain road for any reason. The wheel becomes slippery in my sweat-logged hands, but I hold my position and drive on.

Still, the birds keep coming and coming, and each time one of those little carcasses hits the windshield, it lands like a blow in the center of my chest. I have to fight the impulse to stop, get out, scoop them all up and save them so they can fly away. That's what she wanted.

learn to fly

fly away

Only I know that I can't. If I stop to save the birds, it'll be a suicide mission, and I've made it too far to give up like that.

I turn on the wipers, sweep off the dead carcasses piled up against the windshield, swallow my own sickness as they tumble onto the road.

I'm sorry, I silently transmit to them as each one hits the pavement behind me.

They keep coming, though, every one identical to the still-alive bird I scooped off the track down at Goofy Golf after the die-off, identical to the one I first killed when it dive-bombed my go-kart on my twelfth birthday.

I take one shaky hand off the wheel, fish around in my jacket pocket for the feather I found stuck inside the cup outside City Hall Station. I spin it between my fingers a few times. I still don't know why this ended up on my Trade Screen. It hasn't helped me in any way, hasn't earned me Ascent Credits or given me extra rations or dropped any of the cool new weps from the expansion pack. For a while I thought it might be a special kind of buff, like an invisible shield or something. But it's not.

This feather hasn't done one thing for me. It's just a useless souvenir.

I open the window an inch or so and let it blow out, flicking my gaze to the side-view mirror to watch it disappear behind me. A tight little lump forms in my throat as it flaps in the wind. Only it's not just one feather anymore; it's two, and they're attached to the body of a bird and just before it hits the ground, it flies off.

I flick my gaze to the rearview mirror, watch as the bird becomes smaller and smaller the higher it flies until it's nothing but a black speck far behind me.

When I turn back to the road, I slam the brakes so hard the Jeep almost careens off the side of the mountain. I pull over, watch as the blackbird carcasses continue to fall, turning gray and dissolving before they touch down.

I crane my neck to look out the window. This must be some kind of screen trick. Stupid Relic; it'll show things sometimes that aren't really there until I toggle the mouse back and forth. But this is no trick. The birds are coming down, their falling bodies disintegrating until all I can see around me are quintillions of subatomic gray particles, and before I know it, I'm sitting on the side of the road, gearshift in neutral, in the middle of a fog so dense I can barely see past the end of the truck.

I lean against the seat and scratch my head. The goggles—Cam's gamer goggles—are right there on my face, just like when I left the house.

Brain spin. Someone's really trying to trip my shit.

NIM. For all I know, there are enemy outposts all around me. If they can control things like earthquakes, then for sure they can control something easy, like weather. And why wouldn't they? They know I can't speed through triple-dense fog. They've got me exactly where they want me, and they want me to fail this one last, crucial time.

I put the truck in gear, ease back onto the road, keep it much slower than I want to. I'll never make it through this fog on these roads if I don't maintain near-crawling speeds, but that's also what makes me 1200 percent vulnerable. It's a calculated risk that I have to take, because this time plan B does not exist.

The fog congeals, and I back off the gas even more. The Relic continues to play screen tricks on me, flash-framing gray-scale chunks of Goofy Golf and Napoleon Burger at me between screen grabs of the fog-shrouded trees. I want to trust the map; I really do. I can't throw my hands up in surrender. I know the fog is a block, that they're trying to confuse me, make me quit. But just because I can't see the road doesn't mean I have to give up on the mission.

I take a quick look around the cab to see if there's anything in here I can use—handgun, bazooka, switchblade—which, of course, there isn't. But lined up along the face of the dashboard is an entire panel of knobs, one of which happens to be a radio.

Are you kidding me? How could I not have thought to look for a radio?

I reach out, turn it on, twist the dial looking for a break in the static. But I'm up in the mountains, engulfed in air so superdense I can barely see—I mean, what are my chances of getting a signal up here?

I hit the scan button anyway and let it run. Blips of words out of context pop out at me through the radio: a pebble of conversation here, a shard of theological wisdom there.

Know that Jesus loves—

WFIN in Sandusky—all talk, all the—

It makes sense for the noise to come in and out in fragments like that. I mean, nothing will ever be intact the way it was at one time.

I swallow the knot of sickness that pushes into my throat. Negotiate the next curve slower than I have to. Look around. Realize with a jolt that my attention has gone completely into soft focus. I sharpen the view, notice the road has taken a steep downward curve, catch a glimpse of what looks like the shores of Lake Erie through the fog-camouflaged trees. Before I can even register the curved arch of the Cedar Point roller coasters in the dust-choked distance, I'm already off the hill, and while it's not exactly sunny anymore, at least the haze has started to lift some.

The road stretches out long and flat in front of me, and after I quick check the mirrors, I hit the gas and take off like a bat out of hell.

But I don't make it very far.

Down the highway about five or ten miles, the road bucks as if something has slammed against it from deep underground, and before I know it, I'm dodging huge chunks of earth that look like they've been tossed across staggering distances like Styrofoam movie props. Slabs of asphalt lie scattered along the entire length of the road, chunks that the earth must have regurgitated during the recent quakes.

I grip the wheel, swerve like crazy to keep from hitting stuff

big enough to take me out of commission. But the debris is literally everywhere: toppled electrical poles, unnatural land for-
mations, spires of black smoke dotting the landscape, a pile of
wreckage, broken glass, twisted yellow metal. . . .

My hands grip the wheel as I sweat-panic through the obsta-
cles, force myself not to close my eyes against the devastation.

I drop my foot to the floor, gun the engine, cut straight
through a massive plume of black-charred air. For a moment, even
with the goggles on, I'm blinded by the choking sting of smoke
that has engulfed me.

I can't let it suck me in. I gotta power through, man.

Power through, or die trying.

- 25.5 -

I swipe at the rivulets of sweat dripping down my face—only it's not sweat, it turns out. It's tears.

I need a platoon.

I need a mapper and a healer.

I need cc's.

But I've got nothing.

It's just me.

Caleb Tosh.

I've never been more alone.

- 26 -

The sky is coated in a brown-gray film.

Occasionally a radio station comes in clear enough to hear music or talking, but it's just a blip or two before the signal is lost again. I keep it on scan anyway, in case something comes through eventually—some minuscule reassurance, at least, that I'm headed in the right direction.

As if on cue, the static coughs itself to life, and for a few seconds, it's a battle between bits of music versus sound bites of conversation. When it finally settles on music, I lean forward in disbelief.

It's Ravyn. It's the song Ravyn sang at the Castle, when she started with the melody and Eek joined in and something about the words had wrapped so tightly around me I couldn't breathe. It moved me that day, listening to her sing. I *felt* something. Something real. For the first time since my mom climbed into the bug truck with Stan.

And I know how crazy it sounds, but that song is playing on the radio right now, and it's her singing it, I swear. I'd know Ravyn's voice anywhere.

"That was the Prophets with their latest track, entitled—"

I strain to hear the name, but the DJ's voice sputters and falls away.

I start panic-mashing the buttons on the panel, trying to find the song again through all the static. My gaze shifts between the radio and the road until I finally have to accept that the radio is pretty much useless at this point.

The truck feels less and less steady the longer I drive.

I scan the horizon for signs of battle.

The air is full of the crackle and sulfur of unleashed rage.

The road stretches out long and vacant in front of me, and my eyes slip in and out of focus. My head still hurts from the blow I took when I was kidnapped by the commandos, and somewhere along the way, the combination of exhaustion and pain starts messing with my head. The highway pixilates, blurring bits of shape and color in the space in front of me until I can't distinguish asphalt from landscape anymore. I lift up the yellow goggles, rub my eyes to clear out my vision, but the road keeps narrowing, fills in with traffic. Trees materialize along its edges that weren't there a second ago, and then people and dogs and kids on skateboards, and I swear it looks just like the street in Sandusky, Ohio, where I live.

Up ahead, a small yellow pixel appears right smack in the middle of my line of vision. It performs an act of mitosis, splitting once, then splitting again and again until it comes into full view in the shape of a bug truck.

Only then does it begin to close in on me; and just as it passes by, frame by stuttering frame, Stan the Bug Man turns and stares at me, and so does my mom. Shadows and light fall across her face as she watches me over her shoulder.

I call out for her.

But they keep going, speeding the wrong way down a one-way street, and her face washes out, and so does the Termi-Pest logo on the truck's siding; and just as I swing forward again, hands gripping the wheel, ready to spin the truck around and go after them, a mortar round hits the road ahead of me, then another, blowing a hole in the asphalt big enough to swallow me and the Jeep whole.

I jerk the wheel to keep from falling into it, but the movement is too quick, too uncontrolled. I start flipping, flipping, more times than I can count. By the time the truck stops rolling, I'm sure I've been ejected, that I'm bleeding out on the side of the road.

Something inside me isn't right. I can feel it. Like someone hit the kill switch, and now the signal between my brain and my road-thrashed body has been sheared off at the core.

I try to move, but I can't.

Can't get my eyes to open.

Can't talk.

Can't even hear myself think over the sound of all the air traffic.

Wait a minute. . . . What's with all the air traffic?

I squint my eyes, get them to open to little slits, just enough to make out a sky full of Chinooks and Harriers and F-16 fighter jets. Some of them shoot rounds toward the ground; they are instantly returned, which means there must be tanks or brigades amassed along the side of the road, engaging them.

I'm lying half dead right in the middle of the Battle of UpRising, and I have nothing left to fight with.

"*T-Man!*"

It's all I can do to keep my eyes open, let alone focus on who's calling my name.

"You're still in it! Your platoon's holding off mobs of infiltrators, but they can't keep them down much longer. If you can get to the tunnels, you're in. You're ready to Ascend, dude. Ascend!"

I'm having trouble squaring the sound of Cam Tyler's voice with the sight of his toon, Tyco, kneeling on the ground next to me. All I know is, there are no tunnels. I can't Ascend now.

"It's a trap," I tell him, the words semistuck inside my mouth.

"No, it's not!" He grabs me by the arm of my coat and tries to hoist me up. "Doomstalkers has 12/12 for UpRising. We got full rezzes and heals, and Deathtoaliens found the entrance to Turk's lair!"

He doesn't understand. Turk just passed me in his bright yellow Termi-Pest truck going the other way. He's not in the tunnels anymore. He's not anywhere anymore.

She was with him.

And they were going the wrong way.

Another mortar round hits too close for comfort. Rocks and

debris scud all around us, but I can't make myself get out of the line of fire.

"You've got full weps and max damage," Tyco screams. "God-dammit, Tosh, if you don't launch, you're gonna draw aggro and we'll be—"

The ground is rocked by explosion. I raise my hand to block out the lethal brightness of a helicopter bursting apart in a mid-air cataclysm of fire and smoke. Tunnel raiders stagger down the highway in flames; others scream against the agonizing strikes of machine-gun rounds as they drop like bugs in an extermination death march.

It's gonna be another wipe.

I drag myself to a sitting position while Tyco geeks out nearby, hopping around, shouting orders at me to "Level" and "Ascend." Something quick-whizzes next to my head, and the next thing I know, Tyco collapses onto the road next to me.

I look around to see who took him out, watch in horror as infiltrators pour out of every abandoned, burnt-out, decaying building and onto the highway. They are fully loaded with weps and max damage, follow shoot-to-kill orders on UpperWorld sol-diers and tunnel raiders, who fly through the air spurting blood and profanity as they die.

Just down the road, an anti-aircraft tank nose-dives into one of the craters laid open by mortar fire. Behind it, the convoy slams its collective brakes, and the panicked shriek of metal on metal pierces straight through the chaos of battle. Too late. The tanks and Jeeps crash into one another, triggering an explosive collision of chassis and fire and smoke and glass. I throw my arm up, shield my face from the fiery blast wave that follows.

The world goes deafeningly silent.

Flaming embers, wisps of charred debris, spirals of blackened smoke rain down from the sky, fall all around me without a trace of sound.

Everyone.

Everything.

Gone.

– 26.5 –

The blackbird just lay there on the go-kart track, flapping its little wings like it was begging someone to notice it wasn't dead.

I don't understand why it had to go and die. I mean, it must have known that someone was coming to save it. Otherwise, why would it have fought so hard? What good does it do to stay alive through all the crap stuff only to give up right at the end, just when things are about to turn around?

– 27 –

The only thing moving are the pyres of smoke rising up all around me.

Every car, truck, and tank is upended; every helicopter a smoldering hull of fuselage on the ground.

Soldiers and commandos alike, all dead. Even Tyco.

I'm sprawled out in the dust and rubble of complete and total loss. Not bleeding the way I thought I would be. Nothing seems broken.

Except that everything seems broken. There isn't a square inch of me that doesn't ache with defeat.

I drag myself across the crumbling landscape, grab on to the fender of an overturned delivery truck, pull myself vertical. Try to absorb the totality of destruction.

My messenger bag is lying a few feet away. I move slowly, gather up the scattered socks and underwear, my phone charger, the gum pack—excruciatingly aware that whatever's in this bag is all there is.

I stumble backward, fall against the delivery truck, press myself into the cool metal siding. Snot and tears drip down my face, catch in the grooves of the roll-up door, trail down the side of it as I collapse to the ground, sputter-crying the way people do when they're sure no one is there to hear them.

You can't help us, and we can't help you.

No one can save you.

I wipe my face on my sleeve, lift my head up, let my gaze coast down the demolished highway. Familiar voices echo in the distance, drift toward me in jagged puffs of smoke.

You've got full weps and max damage.

Save it.

Yeah . . .

I gulp small pockets of fresh air, edge forward, pick my way through the twisted bumpers, cracked guardrails, strips of steel-belted radial tires littering the road.

My shoulders square as I cough through the dense wall of smoke closing in on me, wince at the stench of burnt rubber and axle grease and barbecued engine parts that hang heavy all around me. I throw off the yellow-tinted goggles, not caring about the sting in my eyes without that protection.

As I wave the thick smoke from my face, I see Haze standing a few feet away from me in his ski cap and sunglasses. His face mask is lying at my feet.

I cast a squinted look down the street, then back the other way, but the road in front of me looks strangely, unexpectedly, the way it always has. Calm. Almost serene. No helicopters. No tanks. No gaping mortar holes in the road. Just kids and dogs and weeds growing through cracks in the sidewalks and cars driving past this exact spot where one month ago at ten minutes to four, Stan turned the wrong way down a one-way street and head-on collided with an unsuspecting Jeep before wrapping around a power pole.

But even the site of impact looks unfairly normal. The spray of broken glass is gone now. The flames are gone. The smoke is gone.

Everything.

Gone.

As if it never happened.

As if my mom never existed.

"Tosh," Haze says, real low and slow. "Let go, man."

I look down, see my fingers gripped around the door handle of a bright yellow Termi-Pest truck.

"I have to," I tell him. "He took her, Haze. She's waiting for someone to rescue her."

"You can't," he says. "She's gone, Tosh."

I swallow against the blistering knot in my throat that dissolves my words as I say them.

"How do you begin to process 'does not exist'?"

He shakes his head.

A murmur of activity rises up around us, and I pivot my gaze in time to see the old man darting down the road toward me. Only something bolts him in place a few feet out: maybe the look on my face, or the sight of the bug truck behind me, or the lightning crack of realization that my uncharacteristically irrational decision to run away and his uncharacteristically rational decision to come after me have led him directly to ground zero. He scratches his well-developed pony keg through the deteriorating fabric of his shirt before taking a few clumsy steps back the way he came. *That's right, go home,* I say inside my head. *Take care of Devin. He needs you.*

As I scroll back toward Haze, my eye catches on a pair of black Chuck Taylors moving across the street.

I zoom in on the shoes, work up to the cuffed jeans, to the SUPERGIRL T-shirt, to the sheen of sadness on the girl's face.

Haze follows my line of vision.

"She's okay, just so you know," he says. "Her Jeep got totaled, but she didn't get hurt too bad."

My head goes full-tilt fog for a moment. Fog so thick it blocks out sound. Blocks out everything.

"You probably don't remember any of that."

Haze moves forward as he talks, unwraps my fingers from around the door handle of the bug truck. He opens the door, locks it from the inside, clicks it shut, soft but firm, as I turn and watch the girl, as I count her steps to the corner, as she crosses the street toward us, as she leaves a bundle of fresh flowers not ten feet away from me, next to a bunch of other bundles in various stages of life or death. She kneels down, and I watch her lips moving, and I can't tell if she's praying or not, but it doesn't matter. The sight of her lips raining invisible words over the flowers she brought shocks me out of my daze.

Haze quietly slips my messenger bag from me, pulls the strap over his head as I keep staring.

Mason?

She stands up, tries to smile, but her eyes look like pictures of the earth from outer space, full of clouds and water.

I look down, count the bouquets of flowers—same number as the number of days since my mom left.

Since she died.

My mom.

Died.

A soft burst of wind lifts the hair from around Mason's face, and I want to acknowledge her kindness somehow, but I can't. I can't move or talk or think. I can't . . .

I can't breathe.

"It wasn't anyone's fault," she says. "It was just an accident."

No, I think. The go-karts were an accident. This was a choice. This was 1,586 choices that all could have been made differently if there were a way to turn back time. That's what she wanted. It said so in her note.

"I wish I could," Mason says, as if she read my thoughts. "Go back and change things. But it doesn't work that way."

I know it doesn't. I know it doesn't work that way. Some battles just have to be fought. No heals. No rezzes. No special weps. Just getting from one map through the next, pushing forward, until it doesn't feel like the end is quite so near.

It's symbolic. The indestructible exoskeleton. The almost transcendental will to live.

I look up in time to catch sight of a murmuration of starlings ascend into the sky, watch as thousands of blackbirds shift and spread and twist in an impossibly fragile yet beautiful dance. And just when it seems the birds are going to lose track of each other, to fall away in chaos, they pull back together as if by some internal, magnetic force.

It'd be great if we all had that kind of compass. No one would ever have to worry about finding their way back, no matter how lost they got.

A strange kind of feel-good bruise comes over me, but it's the kind of pain that has substance, that lets you know there's something to it. I lift a shaking hand and press it against my chest. I expect it to pass straight through a mess of broken panes, kicked-out bricks, rusted, bent rebar into a hollowed-out space inside me.

Instead my palm lays out flat against the rise and fall of my rib cage, and I feel the steady beat of my own heart.

Acknowledgments

I could not have negotiated the map of writing this book on my own. I had a posse of CCs and healers, had platoons that flanked me or mapped for me so I could beat the mission and not wipe, who donned the gas mask and rode shotgun when I lost sight of the vision, the road, or the faith. There would be no *Boneyard* without the support of these stellar people, and so, with gratitude as undying as an UnderWorld cockroach, I thank the following:

Erin Murphy, who has withstood approximately 312 weeks of Send Your Agent a Neurotic Email Days and never gave up on this story, even when it was as dismantled as an abandoned amusement park; Liesa Abrams, who saw something between the surreal lines and spaces of Tosh's world that genuinely resonated with truth and beauty for her; e.E. Charlton-Trujillo, for asking that first question ("so tell me about this thing you're writing"), for never sugarcoating her opinion, and for friendship so far above the call of duty it requires its own category; Rachel Watson, for talking me through the initial landscape of the game (to the point of hanging butcher paper from a door and literally drawing out a map of the Boneyard so I could visualize it); Joel Watson, who processed the initial story idea with me so thoroughly I felt like I knew Caleb Tosh to his core by the time I started writing out his story; Tom Watson, who said the exact right combination of words that got me to understand what Tosh's journey really was (even if we were talking about something entirely different at the time)—this manuscript would have stayed in the kill file had it not been for that conversation; Fran Gordon (you know Dad is smiling at us, right?); Lynne Bercaw (my SSPCH); Jennifer Salas (*mi* Chiquita Banana); Doug "Sure-I'll-read-another-draft" Marshall; Erin Murphy's Dog: Mike Jung, Ruth McNally Barshaw, Jeannie Mobley-Tanaka, Deborah Underwood, Kristin Wolden Nitz, Arthur A. Levine, and Conrad Wesselhoeft—Dawgs, your unfailing love and support have literally saved me—I'm deeply grateful for every single one of you (*en boca al coniglio*—arooooo!!); the entire EMLA Gango—the best book champions ever, and not just for me but every one of our agency siblings, in ways that make me sob with joy. And finally, special Ascent Credits to Joshua McCune and Susan Vaught, who were unquestioningly part of the Boneyard Expansion Pack.

And to those who were kind enough (or crazy enough) to read drafts and share their thoughts along the way: Austin Rist (you should be on here at least three times), Carol and John Watson, Doug Marshall, e.E. Charlton-Trujillo, Fran Gordon, Gwendolyn McIntyre (rest in peace, beautiful soul), Jeannie Mobley-Tanaka, Jennifer Salas, Joel Watson, Joshua McCune, Leigh Purtill, Lisa Gus, Lynne Bercaw, Missy Neal, Naheed Hasnat, Pennie Baxter,

Rachel Watson, Ruth and Charlie Barshaw, Sheri Eichar, Sofie Bercaw, Susan Vaught.

Each of us must negotiate our own internal landscape of pain and struggle—and yes, the journey can be challenging, the pain can be brutal, the loneliness, the fear, the isolation can feel surreal at times. But hang tough, my friend. Find your tribe, fight for yourself, be brave, and trust that you'll come out on the other side with more of yourself than you had when you went in.